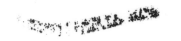

Tanglevine

Library of Congress Control Number 2012934486
Casebound: 978-1-937356-24-8
Trade: 978-1-937356-25-5
Kindle: 978-1-937356-26-2
EPUB: 978-1-937356-27-9

Publisher's Cataloging-in-Publication Data

Shannon, Beth Tashery.
Tanglevine / Beth Tashery Shannon.
p. cm.
ISBN: 978-1-937356-24-8
1. Kentucky—Fiction. 2. Fantasy fiction. 3. Ghost
stories. 4. Murder—Fiction. 5. Detective and mystery
stories. 6. Imaginary places—Kentucky. 7. Love stories.
I. Title.
PS3619.H3549 T36 2012
813.6—dc22
        2012934486

Published by BearCat Press: www.BearCatPress.com

❈ Tanglevine ❈

Beth Tashery Shannon

San Francisco

~ I ~

Awakening

A rustle in the shadows. A commotion of birds. A stone drops into old currents, dim depths stirring, swirling, thirsting, rising.

I struggle upward against the storm. I grapple with the roots that hinder me, the roots that thwart me, the roots that grip me in their talons, the roots that bind me to my bones. Storm sweeps over Tanglevine.

All the leaves howl with human voices.

~ 2 ~

The Blue Grass

O n Sun River a ferry wombles like a beetle fallen in the water. There's the ferryman chewing a piece of cornbread. He lets the breeze do its work, paying no mind at all to what's in his prow. A murdering Domene.

Look at him. The way he commandeers the nose of the boat, boots planted firmly, head lifted, long hair blowing a dark fire. Fine young thorough-bred stallion pawing the deck behind him. Wouldn't you know it? Hard muscles, proud grace, restive eyes. Him and the bay, both. Crossing his chest—the Domene's—a black sash embroidered with fancy silver trim and a long-pointed star. Not just any Domene. One come to lay down the law.

Shy of showing its depths, the river mirrors the palisades, the towering cliffs gleaming grey on the brown water, the woods crowning them like green twilight against the bright sky. Trees cling to the rock faces anywhere roots can finger into a cranny. Here, even the stones are fertile. I try to put words on him, to turn him back, but my mouth is stopped.

Cliff shadow slides over the prow, cloaking the Domene in a shock of cool that makes him glance up. Birds wheel in protest. Scent of damp limestone. Secret dark of river loam. The water gurgles.

The ferry snubs a dock as weathered and peedunky as it is. The Domene glances haughtily at the ferryman's fishing pole propped against a willow, little'uns' toys littering the grass. What'd he expect, a royal welcome from a dozen velvet robed Masters of Twaddle?

Look at him now, waiting by the bay's head as the ferryman struggles with the heavy gangway, never lifting one finger. Who'd think to help a mule pull its load? When all's secure he unleashes that splendor of a stud—the Domene untethers the horse, I mean.

I struggle to touch the horse, to put dread in the smarter of the two. First touch of the dock sends his hooves striking out. Their drumming on the hollow wood echoes up and down the faces of the cliffs as the Domene fights him, jerking his head down. I strain on the horse's side against the enemy to us both, but I'm weak, no muscle no tongue. The Domene has the ferryman fetch a stick and startle him from behind, then forces him to the bank.

My sight dims. The horse swivels his hindquarters, nostrils flaring in alarm, skin flinching like the air's swarming with flies.

Jihan paid the ferryman what he considered fair and swung into the saddle, keeping a short rein. The bay arched its neck in protest at the grip, but tried no more harebrained tricks. He sent it at a canter up the path, following a stream cutting between steep, rocky walls.

His hooves echoed, and Jihan glanced up, knowing the place's bloody history. Three times these stones rang with the clamor of ambush before his great-grandfather finally brought the Blue Grass under Domene control. An obvious death trap, with that overhang and tree cover at the top, but he knew what pressures had tempted the commanders to chance this quickest route. He had felt them, himself.

Not much had changed about frontier war except the frontier. It had advanced eighty miles northward. The Blue Grass Province was now a sleepy backwater, so peaceful he thought nothing of making this final stage of the journey alone, leaving his manservant and armed escort toiling behind with his goods. It was a strangely light feeling, riding alone, attended by no one, responsible for no one.

The narrows opened to a valley of soft grass and early afternoon sunlight. Birds scattered before him, black crows all too familiar from northern battlefields, and the scarlet, crested ones. Wildflowers brushed his mount's knees, butter yellow, white and pleasing shades of purple.

Its formidable south border once crossed, the Blue Grass rolled in gentle pastureland, offering no barriers. Jihan knew its maps like the backs of his hands. Its rich land was inhabited by prosperous farmers and horsemen, an easygoing people who disliked taking orders, treated life and death matters as jokes, and became dangerously serious only over their wagering games. A charming people, but not the most reliable.

At a fork he took the road east, a broad dirt wagon track with grass beside it for riding. His mount was now in a playful mood, flashing its forelegs at butterflies. Maybe it knew it had come home.

He had sold his best battle charger for this flighty thoroughbred. It was lighter, faster, cleaner limbed, but wayward as a bat. He liked the fierce steadiness of the charger better. Here, though, a fine thoroughbred was valued above all, and the ability to handle one earned respect. He touched his heels to the bay's sides and was rewarded with a surge of powerful hind-quarters and an extended gallop to swallow the miles.

The pleasantness of these rolling hills dotted with shade trees was undeniable, but this province was worked nothing so intensively as the Gatelands surrounding the entrances to the Caverns.

The Blue Grass furnished mounts, draft animals, hemp and tobacco to all the Domelands, but it could feed many more than it did. It could support populous training camps, administrative and commercial centers and stockpiles, as well as supplying recruits. All this lay—or would, with properly laid and surfaced wagon roads—only two days' march from the frontier.

The only reason others did not see what he saw was that they did not realize what such a base could do for the City. Inertia showed everywhere in the Caverns, in the carelessness and corruption of government and trade, in the petty squabbling among his own Ward class; even the artists gave the City nothing but over-refined repetitions.

Fresh directions were needed. The Domelands must expand. As all knew, the Domed City traded with certain tribes north of the High River and aided them against their rival neighbors.

But most in the City did not know that under Domene guidance the allies had begun to systematically conquer their neighbors. Once that was done, whoever controlled the united territory would have an open way northward. Officially, there was no plan to conquer the City's allies. But to a frontier commander with friends on City Council, two and two made four.

What the Council refused to see was that their policy was doomed to failure. Once, the Councilors would have listened to the son of Edwarn Master of the Outlands. Now they behaved as if he only wished to foul their plans. Nothing was left to his family but enough wealth for decency and an empty title. Ward Jihan son of Edwarn, field commander in a nonexistent war, had no power to sway the Council.

He had called on his last resource, family ties, to corner the Council Master alone. Mirabil had cleverly strategized the informal feast, using fine wines and gentle maneuvers to relax the Master into reminiscence. Then she lured the

Master's wife to the inner house, leaving Jihan
alone with his guest.

They took a stroll along the outer
colonnade. It was Jihan's favorite private spot,
where the cavern lake stretched dark, mirroring
the lamplit archways of the house, and above
them the filigree of the windows, and soaring
high over all, the scallops, pipes and turrets of
the stalactites.

"My troops have taken the north bank of
the High River from Eagle Rocks to Old
Factory," Jihan said.

"I know." The Council Master smiled.
"Recognition cannot come yet, but it will."

"It's not that. My soldiers are tribal. That
disturbs me. It seems to me that I am training
our future enemies."

"They think we mean to take all for
ourselves?"

"I think we do."

The Master lifted an eyebrow at his
bluntness. When Jihan refused to lower his eyes
he acknowledged with a slight smile. They
strolled on, their reflections appearing and disap-
pearing between the archways, the Master's
azure robes and his own garnet red, and the gold
wine cups in their hands, like jewels thrown into
the deep water. Jihan took his chance. "We need
our own men in the North, In numbers."

"You know the logistical difficulties."

"With respect, Ward Master, the river is wide, but as I said, in places we hold both sides. The only real difficulty is the distance between High River and the Command Center. A century ago, we needed a massive army presence near the Caverns. Now, all the Domelands are our protection. The Caverns are not in easy reach of any who could attack us. If we mean to expand northward, we must relocate the Command Center nearer to our objective. The best access to the High River is from the Blue Grass."

"Agreed." The Master returned readily. "But that poses yet another difficulty. Or, to be precise, two difficulties: the Blue Grass Provincials and the Blue Grass Provincial Government."

"Which of those daunts us?"

The Master ignored his challenge. "You propose drastic changes to the most traditional province in the Domelands. The Blue Grass horse breeders are not your Northern savages. They may cling to a backward way of life, but they can affect Domelands trade, and they know it."

"They are farmers, practical people. They will accept the realities. Especially if their cooperation profits them."

"Conflict might be prevented with astute management," the Master agreed. "But from Governor Fidric?" He lifted an open palm slightly, the elegant hint of a shrug. "Unlikely, to say the least. And what he does not control, he and his cronies obstruct. I scarcely need remind you of what Old Guard opposition can do."

No, he did not need reminding. His father had dreamed of a paved road, a Great Road to connect the Caverns with all the provinces. Goods could be moved along it with speed and safety in wagons under Domene merchants' direct supervision, and people would be more willing to leave the crowded Caverns, to settle in the provinces. With difficulty, his father had won consent for the project. Jihan's own assignment had been to provision the work crews. It was his first command.

He remembered all too well. The explosions eviscerating the night, the screams as the ground upended, crushing men and horses. A severed arm falling from the air into his lap. His lieutenant blinded for life. His desperate retrieval of the survivors through a wall of fire. And in the cold morning, the miles of devastation, each shattered paving stone mocking all his father's hopes and years of labor.

The saboteurs were disgruntled caravanners, it was suspected. That was never proved, but it was clear who had incited them. Within six months the Old Guard had ousted his father and seized control of the Office of the Outlands. Jihan knew very well what the Old Guard could do.

They reached the end of the colonnade. In the water, the reflected constellations of lighted windows shimmered beneath the hanging formations. The Master remarked, "There are suitable locations for a base north of the High River, I understand?"

"There are. And at this rate we'll hold those firmly enough in twenty years."

"I fear that I agree." The Council Master did not hide his regret. Jihan saw how powerfully he wanted to be the one to conquer the Northlands.

Jihan turned the full force of his own desire on him. "Give me the Blue Grass. I'll give you your base."

The Master's laugh was harsh. Quickly he cut it off, turning away out of politeness. "Forgive me, Ward Jihan, but your youth shows. Only the Council can remove a provincial governor. If they did, surely they would wrangle for a year, then appoint some innocuous compromise...which hardly describes you."

"Let Fidric remain Governor of the Blue Grass. Give me the means to his treasury."

The Master raised his cup to drink, but then lowered it. "Master of Revenues?" He smiled slightly. "Your information is correct, he is retiring." He frowned into the water, considering. "You would give up your command for a third tier civil post?"

"To start with."

"What you propose would not be easy. Nor would you accomplish it all in a day."

"I know."

The Master studied him closely. "I have always thought your ambition to regain your family's honor commendable." But frowning again, he gazed across the lake at the small lights of a neighboring estate. At last he said, "Unorthodox means will find no official support."

He had chosen the words with fastidious care. Jihan liked them. "I understand."

"Then this is our bargain, Jihan son of Edwarn. I will appoint you Master of Revenues in the Blue Grass, but that is all I will do. The rest is up to you. Gain me the province, and I promise you the resources for your base."

His base. Jihan smiled again at all that this implied. The dangers were clear. Fail to gain control, and end up buried in provincial administration. Do it clumsily, and be sacrificed to

Council politics. But succeed, and become the only man in the position to found...a beginning with no limits. In the Caverns his family was now enduring gossip about him, some enemy's invention of hushed-up misconduct on the frontier and a demotion, but his father and Mirabil knew the truth. The fewer others who did, the better. Especially, in the Blue Grass. Not yet. Not until he gained the leverage to act openly.

I shin through a window but Fared's there before me. He smiles. "I unlocked the door, silly."

He's made us a nest in the straw, got a quilt and a lantern all darked except for one pane of light. Horses shift and whuff in their stalls and the one lantern beam makes Sunlight of his dandelion hair. It turns his slender body all to molten gold.

"Look at you," I say and hurry greedily into his arms. We tug off my clothes any old how and then oh! his chest glides hot against my nipples and his thighs slide strong between mine. He knows to clap his hand over my mouth. My cry tastes of his palm, dusty salty taste of horse sweat. Fared's my cousin, already part of me. Our parents say someday

they'll dance at our wedding but we're still way too young.

We're not! We know love is wide as the sweep of the wind, forever as the circling of the Sun. We already have what they want to keep from us, joy beyond human knowing. We drink each other in kisses so thirsty it's a wonder he doesn't end up in my skin and me in his.

Fared, gold Fared drenched in tiny freckles, don't I love you, and don't I, and don't I? Looking in his eyes I scoonch my back down into the quilt, unfurling for him like petals within petals. He kisses me everywhere he can reach.

The horses start awake. Fared raises his head. "What's that?"

Feet. Many feet. The tramping of feet fills the whole village circle. As many as hail stones clashing, banging, echoing off the faces of the houses and shops. The window goes dusky brown, then red with a wrath of torches. As we rush to look out, the yelling starts.

Soldiers. Domene soldiers, hundreds of them. "They've broke through," I whisper, but it's not real. They fill the village circle like ants seething on an anthill, swords and metal armor glaring in the torchlight like the fury they say churns in the bowels of the earth. With slit eye visors, barred mouths, nightmare no-faces, they swarm the houses, boiling like ants crawling on ants, dragging people out in their nightclothes, in nothing at all, herding screaming people, knocking those who fight them to the ground beneath their trampling boots.

"They're after my daddy." Fared yanks on his pants and grabs a pitchfork. I know he's right, but I try to hold him back. He shakes free and he's gone, darting along shadowed porches for the lane where he lives.

I snatch my clothes and dress, hardly daring to look away. Soldiers part for a horseback officer and for just an instant I can see my house across the village circle. The door gapes black. The Domenes have got them! I can't see them among the red of the torches and the grappling, I can't see them anywhere.

Fared races from the shadows of the farrier's yard toward his lane. Some Domenes spot him, take after him. For two heartbeats I think he's slipped them, but they tackle him to the ground. The pitchfork clatters useless under him. One jerks up his head by the hair. The officer on the horse signals the soldiers to make way, and another horseman rides through, one without armor.

It's Cob Snows from Leatherhand. What's he doing with them? How can he stare down at Fared's face like that? He nods and calls to the

Domene commander. Fared fights like a demon-possessed wildcat but they heave him off his feet, carrying him by the arms and legs. Shouts sound, and the neighbors surge to his aid. Domenes fall, but they cluster around Fared, letting nobody near. They haul him to the wall of Hemmie's kiln.

They make him face the wall.

Grabbing a shovel I charge for them slashing.

At a village of limestone houses roofed with turf Jihan watered his horse. Craftspeople in their porches and farmers in wagons nodded politely, eyeing his ornate sash and inlaid scabbard with curiosity and his horse with envy.

One or two of the women also eyed him. The boldness of Blue Grass women was proverbial. It was said they took what lovers they would, and the men did not even try to curb them. A shadowy haired beauty took him by surprise, leaning over a window sill to smile down at him. Jihan returned a courteous nod and faced forward. He was no prude, but uncontrolled desires opened one to others' control.

A gaggle of children gathered to watch the bay drink. He heard their tittering behind him, and caught a whisper that no Domene could manage such a horse.

As he remounted, a pebble smacked the bay's rump. Jihan toed the far stirrup just in time. Wheeling the horse, he spotted the culprit, a little ruffian about the age of his younger son. It was hard not to smile.

It was good to see children well fed, whole, unmarked by the terrors of war. He gave the boy a stern look and they all scattered, reminding him of the red crested birds.

The afternoon sun weighed hot as he pressed on for Arcadia. The children's Domene-baiting put the beauty's smile in perspective. She might like his looks, but that was all. These people traded, paid their taxes, but resisted Domene ways.

They had taken decades to conquer, so united by their strange muddle of nature worship and magic that it had been necessary to eliminate their oracle-priest and his heirs. After that, resistance had crumbled, and the war was soon over.

Bringing order to the province had required harshness at first, but gradually the old beliefs that fired their stubbornness had faded, leaving only vague superstitions. They still had quite a collection of odd customs, by all accounts, and clung to their disorderly eccentricities with a pride that was hard to fathom.

Many Domenes mistook lack of civilization for stupidity, but Jihan did not. He suspected he would find some few here who were as able as any in the Caverns. In fact, his plan depended on it.

His shadow slanted before him as at last he ascended a hill and saw across a valley of rippling grass a steeper rise topped by a long stone rampart. Its high walls were pierced by slots for archers and broken only by a single portal. Arcadia.

Never had Jihan seen such an old fashioned fortress except in pictures. Something deep in him, some remnant of his boyhood love of old tales and history, soared at the prospect of building his power in this place where so many renowned warriors and commanders had earned their fame long ago. He urged his mount to a final surge of speed.

~ 3 ~
Arcadia

ne grabs me from behind, lifting me off my feet. I jab the shovel into his shin and he roars, but other hands seize me, wrench the shovel away, spin me to face a visor with a single narrow slit eye and grid for a mouth. A blow puts the torches out, and the ground rushes up to hit my face.

Like waking, but the nightmare's the same. I lie on the grass, boots stepping over me. Bruises throb where some have kicked me. Grace's house is burning, and April's shop. Fared stands by the wall of the kiln, and my other cousins, the twins Gilly and Robin, and little Jay crying.

The Domene commander shouts at Aunt Cyntha. "Where is your husband?" he demands. "Give us your false prophet. Now! Or your children go into the kiln."

This isn't waking. It can't be. I've been knocked clean out of the world the Sun has made into chaos shadows, fever dreams, misshapen un-things that aren't. The Sun wouldn't let them be real.

A soldier slings little Jaybird up roughly. Aunt Cyntha claws him and the neighbors cry out with her, but they're three dozen and unarmed against three hundred swords. I elbow myself off the grass, going for a carelessly held sword, but I'm dizzy and the night turns over and over like a barrel rolled down a hill. A soldier pins my arms.

"Let my children go. Here I am." *But the man who pushes to the front of the captives isn't Uncle Tyree, it's Yarrow Lees. They look alike, a little, both with coppery hair, descendants of the first Heron, Wisteria. And if the Domenes only knew it, Yarrow's fought them just as bravely as my uncle.*

The commander eyes Yarrow coldly. But he doesn't have to decide. Uncle Tyree steps from the shadows between two houses. He faces them tall, unarmed, calm. He's walking to his death and he knows it. "My life for theirs," *he says. He points at the village, too.* "All of them."

No! the neighbors yell, but my uncle only looks at them.

There'll another Heron, *his look says. I catch his glance at Berry the saddler and realize he's named her, she'll be Heron after he's gone.*

Her look answers, clearer than words, as long as there's a Blue Grass, the Sun will love it.

The Domene gives my uncle a single nod in that strange slow way of theirs. "Your offer is accepted. Upthegrove will be spared."

Then the world goes insane. They leap on my uncle, plunging their swords into him. Blood sprays. The neighbors scream, jumping on the Domenes bare handed, fighting, grappling, biting. Uncle Tyree falls in his blood. He dies without a word.

The commander signals to the men holding his family. He'll honor his word. They say Domenes at least do that.

But they cut Robin down where he stands, and Gilly falls on top of him. I can't see Aunt Cyntha and Jay, only a swarm of soldiers, hacking, stabbing. Fared wrestles with one until a sword sweeps a glaring arc.

In the flickering light Fared's body falls one way and his head the other. I scream and scream. The Domene gripping me laughs.

Arcadia's old stone walls looked as sound as if it were still a fortress. They were so massive that the portal Jihan rode through was a short tunnel.

Within lay a wide, square courtyard. On all four sides an enclave rose in narrow clusters against the walls, like the buildings of the Domed City that climbed the sides of the cavern chambers. Other touches of home were the carving surrounding the doors and stone lattices on the windows.

No inscriptions identified the Governor's Residence or Departmental offices—a defense from the old days. If the enemy entered he would lose his momentum in uncertainty, but Jihan was annoyed at being in the same position. He had thought to be watched for and greeted. The place was lax. The courtyard was empty. Most Domenes preferring to shelter from heat and glare, all the doors were shut and the curtains drawn.

Only in the south corner was there activity, a string of horses in a fenced enclosure with a few Outlanders moving among them. A caravan unloading. That would be the Department of

Trade. The Department of Revenues must be nearby. Jihan rode over.

Five caravan riders jingled, thumped and chattered, their speech a gamut like their sturdy breeches, shirts and trinkets in many colors, and their knives and swords in the styles of several lands. Sunlight flashed from the feathers and bells decorating both horses and riders. A grey man and young woman with a disfiguring scar sorted cargo as a tall black man and scrawny waif unbuckled chests and bags.

The fifth would be the leader. He could read. Head bent over a book of lading, he counted and marked off. Jihan drew rein outside the enclosure. "Health to you. Which is the Office of Revenues?"

The leader turned, tossing back a coppery mane. Jihan had the impression of a hawk nose, full lips, and a dizzy abyss, the blue that draws the gaze between the clouds. An emptiness like falling.

But the eyes flicked over him, sizing up his tanned skin and Outlander clothes, his long hair, trim beard and sash, and Jihan realized his first impression was wrong. No fool, the man returned a bow of the head, Domene fashion. "Water's over there." The lazy consonants and savored vowels were pure Blue Grass.

So was the rebuke. As firmly as the difference in their ranks allowed, the caravan leader was reprimanding him for the bay's sweating and blowing. Perhaps not unreasonably. In his eagerness to arrive, he had ridden hard for such a hot day. But he had yet to receive an answer to his question. He waited.

The caravanner returned glance for glance, then shrugged and tipped his head toward the next cluster of buildings.

"Thank you. Kindly send word that the Master of Revenues has arrived."

Dismounting, Jihan led his horse to the trough beneath a spreading tree. Regarding the locals, his initial plan was simple. Intelligent Outlanders were more useful than lackbrains, Domene or otherwise. The Domed City was doomed to stagnation unless it recognized able Outlanders, even as far as adding seats to the Council itself—a heresy to many Domenes, and not only of his class.

He made his stance clear by accepting the man's advice. He let the bay plunge its lips into the water for a brief drink, then since no groom appeared, he walked it himself in a cooling circle in the shade.

As he allowed it a second drink he saw the caravan leader, boot toe propped on the fence, considering him. He had startled him. Good. "Arn," the leader's voice carried over the stone pavement, "go shake a groom awake."

The door of the Department of Revenues opened. The bay raised its head, dribbling water over Jihan's sleeve as four men crossed the pavement toward him, robes rippling in the breeze, hair flowing to shoulders where embroidered hoods were gracefully laid, their faces and hands as untainted by the sun as if they had never left the Caverns. Their stately approach paid him due respect, if belatedly. His mount snorted at their billowing, but the scrawny rider hurried forward. Jihan tossed him the reins.

The officials bowed their heads deeply. "Health to you, Ward Jihan. Your presence honors Arcadia."

Jihan acknowledged with an equally gracious nod. It was the eldest who had spoken, a tall man whose white beard fell like a fine veil over his sash, but all the sashes were grey, blazoned only with a simple silver border. Oddly, all were only clerks.

His predecessor had already returned to the Caverns, but the next in command, an Assessor Waldis son of Willim, should welcome him. It seemed the Blue Grass Department of Revenues was even more disorganized than his inquiries in the Caverns had suggested. "Health to you," Jihan returned. "I wish to speak with the Assessor before I rest. Is he within?"

He caught a quick glance among them. The scrawny caravan rider walked his horse in a small circle, staying within hearing.

Something was amiss.

"Show me my headquarters," Jihan suggested. With disquieting alacrity the clerks conducted him to privacy, through a dim entrance hall to a reception chamber hung with tapestries woven in the Caverns.

There the tax collectors awaited him, and the under-clerks. All bowed their heads silently, as if expecting no more than his nod as he passed. Whatever the matter was, it seemed all Arcadia knew of it.

The four senior clerks ushered him to an office with a massive desk of dark wood and book cases to the ceiling. Curtains of dull gold muted the afternoon harshness and flames flickered in lamps hanging from chains. Jihan motioned for them to shut the door and advanced on them. "Well?"

"Assessor Waldis has been missing for seven days, Ward."

That startled him into silence.

It did not sort with what he had learned of the Assessor. Waldis was fifty years old, inactive, inoffensive, and loathe to venture farther from the Office of Revenues than his fellow officials' card parties. "Say on."

"Jame son of Jame," the old man introduced himself, "First Clerk. Nine days ago a message arrived from a remote village claiming damages from storms and flooding. They requested adjustments before tax collection. Last week Assessor Waldis and I rode to this Tanglewood."

"Tanglevine," another of the clerks murmured discreetly.

"Tangle*vine*," Jame emended with an edge of irritation, "In the Woodhollow District. That is a poor corner bordering the Eastern Mountains. We had a map, but the way was heavily forested and intolerably rough, and we did not arrive until night. Assessor Waldis heard the farmers' requests for inspections. I drew up a schedule. The next morning, the Assessor began his tour, while I returned for the village's tax roll. The last I saw of the Assessor, he was riding out on inspection with one of the farmers for a guide."

Jihan frowned, not following the reasoning. "You returned to Arcadia, leaving the Assessor alone? Why did you not bring the tax roll with you?"

No one seemed eager to answer. A short, balding clerk at last shouldered the burden. "Tanglevine's records had not been located, Ward."

"I see. You also took no guard?"

"It was not a tax collection. We had nothing to rob. But for the severity of the claims, a single under-clerk could have handled the matter."

Jihan lifted a hand in noncommittal acceptance. "And?"

"The village's tax roll still eluded us, but the Assessor would need an assistant. Thinking a younger man might serve him better, I sent Third Clerk Hadlin." Jame indicated a dark haired man with almond eyes. Jihan turned to him.

"I lost my way, Ward," Hadlin admitted. "I spent the night in another village where I got more fleas than sleep. A local offered to guide me, but then the oaf merely showed me a muddy path and pointed the way. When at last I reached Tanglevine, the innkeeper told me Assessor Waldis was gone. He had paid his bill and ridden away two days before. Why, or where, she did not know. I thought he must have returned to Arcadia, so I went to the stable to order my horse saddled again." The clerk's look was a plea.

Jihan encouraged him to go on with silent attention.

"That is when I saw the Assessor's saddle," he asserted.

"At Tanglevine," Jihan made sure of what the young man was claiming. "In the inn stable?"

"Yes, Ward." Hadlin glanced at the others. "And I *am* sure it was his—light brown leather, tooling on the girth, and on the left flap the star of the City."

"None of us believed him at first," Jame admitted. "Who would dare harm a City official? But that was three days ago. The Assessor is still missing."

"They claimed no knowledge of any saddle," Hadlin added. "When I tried to show them, it was gone. Everyone I questioned repeated the same tale, the Assessor had ridden away, leaving the inspections unfinished."

"So you returned to Arcadia?"

"I was only one man, and they were pressing about the inspections—they thought we should simply continue as if nothing had happened!"

Because of the young man's distress Jihan ignored his loss of self-control. "Have you sent out search parties?"

"Yes, Ward. The Governor lent us men. They have all returned," Jame answered. "No

trace of the Assessor could be found on the
roads, or in Tanglevine." Jame turned a hand
palm upward. "As your skills in such matters far
surpass ours, and you were due any day…"

Jihan paced to the desk. Its top was clear of
papers and so polished he saw his own face
frowning back at him. He turned. "What of
ransom? Any hint of a demand?"

Hadlin looked startled. "No, Ward."

Jame cleared his voice. "Excuse my boldness,
Ward Jihan, but I have served in this province
for thirty years. The villagers of Tanglevine are
underfed, ignorant, scrabbling for a bare living.
They play no subtle game of clues and ransoms.
Leaving Assessor Waldis' saddle in sight was a
mere blunder. One of them quarreled with the
Assessor over an inspection, or his horse slipped
in the mud, or he died in his sleep, and the
innkeeper thought to profit from his possessions.
If you wish my advice, Ward, put fear into them
and soon enough they will confess what befell.
We have grown too lenient. We are losing their
respect, and now we pay the price. Knowing
what you have done in the North, we have asked
the Governor for a troop of Provincial Guard.
They await your command."

Jihan turned so they would not see the full
force of his annoyance. Stalking to the window

he parted the curtain, flooding the room with the glare of sunset. Storm an impoverished village with an army? What sort of fools were these? "And if the Assessor is alive?" he asked with cold quiet.

"Is there hope of it, Ward?" Hadlin asked forlornly.

"It's possible." In the courtyard each leaf of the tree gleamed red as if with blood. The caravan riders were carrying the last of their cargo through the darkness of an open door. "None of the Provincial Guard are locals?"

That was a rhetorical question, and they knew it. Provincial Guard were Outlanders, but never from the province where they served. In theory, that assured their loyalty. In actuality, Jihan believed it also kept any class of Domene-loyal provincials from growing up to supplant the second rate Domene officials who ran the provinces.

Waldis was his responsibility. His career in Arcadia must not open with an incident. This must be settled quickly and firmly. "Go, one of you, and tell the Master of Trade I wish to speak with him. Say I want to borrow the caravan riders."

"Caravanners, Ward?" Jame rustled audibly. "Those vagabonds are no better than—"

Than a careless old fool who rode into a troubled village without a single swordsman? Or a collection of scribblers who first lost their tax records, then their tax assessor? Jihan contented himself with silently turning and impaling them with his eyes.

One of them bowed his head and hurried out.

~ 4 ~

The Caravan Leader

ream riding. Silver horses beneath a mirror moon. Do things as despicable as Domenes dream? Of what? The dark Caverns they come from? Formations unfurling like fans, eyeless fishes with tails like veils? Of torches' shadows furrowing dead tyrants' stone faces?

In my dream's silver hollow the hoofbeats double. Eight legs flash, two manes flow, fire and shadow like wind over land. Bells' chiming, swords' ringing, mingling with the rush of the waterfall.

Waterclimb, white torrents rise, they flood, they whirl the stars, sharp stars that tear loose the black roots, stars that pulse raw and gleaming as a heart gashed open. Ha, you think I don't know that anguish rising, flooding, mingling with the water? Surging as hope drains away.

In the dim places and the tangle vine places where leaves drown and darkness breathes. Where

*the leaves cover it over, cover it over, cover over.
Cover over the night.*

*In the morning, all the leaves flash rainbows.
The grass breathes diamonds, even the littlest
weeds sing colors. And tiny in each dewdrop, a star.
A prisoner.*

*Sky reaches. I struggle to touch. Sky calls. I
claw to rise, I flail to fly between the clouds, to touch
freedom. My cry rises high and thin as a bird's as I
fall. Darkness slides over. Darkness eats me.*

A bird screeched. Jihan looked up. The sun
rose over a slope crested by a line of trees. Their
sturdy branches stretched into the sky, casting
shadows like fissures in the glittering dew.

The inhuman vitality of the Outlands
always struck him the most at sunrise. The trees
reached for the light with alien purposefulness,
and the dewy grass showed the crisscrossing
paths of rabbits or foxes, roads with secret uses
having nothing to do with the one he traveled
on.

The very stones were clothed with foreign
life, this grass that endured trampling like some
insensate carpet, yet crept slyly, slowly engulfing

the ruins of the ancient cities, obliterating even memory.

The caravanners rode with drowsy eyes, taking for granted the jewelled gleam of each separate hair on every horse.

Jihan doubted they were overjoyed to be called out on this business. They had been due for time off. They showed nothing, but incurious they were not. As they had readied at dawn, he had overheard the black caravanner mutter to the scrawny one, "—they call the Hero of the North? I thought Windland 'as waggling us."

"Not a wiggle. 'S a Ward, to boot."

"An owner of the Domed City? Really? Never seen one of *them* up close before."

Jihan had seen their kind though, and he had learned to respect them on their own ground. Caravanners made the best scouts and trackers.

Jame was right, the riders who transported cargo between the provinces were vagabonds, as likely as not to run black market on the side, but they were capable fighters. Even the women among them were tougher in adverse terrains and weathers than many seasoned soldiers. Some could scarcely endure a roof overhead.

The leader gazed at nothing in particular, the bells in his tall chestnut's mane jingling in time to its trot. Whatever his thoughts were, he had hardly spoken. At thirty Jihan was young for a commander. Windland was younger, but he had the look of a veteran of the roads.

At the Governor's welcoming dinner last night, the Master of Trade had told him the caravan leader was indeed a native of the Blue Grass, the son of a well-off farmer. Surprisingly, he had a Domene wife. Not a Gate City half-caste, a woman of respectable family. She wore the sash of the Halls of Learning, the Master of Trade said—the scholarly Green Order. Jihan's was only the practical Black. It was intriguing.

He squeezed his knees and the bay advanced. The red mare flattened her ears, knowing a troublesome stud when she saw one. Jihan saw the caravan leader's assessing glance at his seat and hands before he gave her a calming word.

"Do you know the road to Tanglevine?"

Again, the disconcerting blue gaze. It was not the color. The caravanner's eyes were actually grey-blue, nothing so vivid as the jay feather in his hair. It was the openness of his regard that threw one off balance, an unfocused wideness as if it held no judgement, no compre-hension even, merely pure, almost preternatural, sight. But then the corners of his mouth indented in an ironic hint of a smile. "I won't get us lost."

So he had heard about the Revenues officers' bumblings. Little surprise, caravan riders always knew more than they were supposed to. "Have you been to this village?"

"Only far as Woodhollow, where the trail branches. We'll reach Tanglevine by late afternoon."

A movement drew Jihan's eye. Beyond a wooden fence a pasture tilted to a willow-shaded stream. Weanling foals streaked across in mad abandon, flagging their short tails. Past that stood a barn, trimmer and more secure than the houses in some lands. Beyond again, an apple orchard. "A fortunate province, yours."

Windland smiled as he watched the foals. "It's favored," was all he allowed, but his voice gave away his affection for his home.

"Yet, my clerks described Tanglevine as poor and struggling."

"We're still in horse country. Woodhollow district's over on the edge, soil's too thin to farm 'cept for the bottoms, and those get flooding."

"Such as the damages Assessor Waldis went to inspect? Are such requests common, then?"

The caravanner finger-combed his mare's mane. "People usually turn to each other before the Fortress." He glanced at Jihan and shrugged. "No offense. Just more chance of help from the neighbors."

"None taken. The Governor and his staff are not very attentive to local concerns, then?" Jihan checked the bay's attempt to bite the mare's neck.

Windland let her swerve aside. "Got a race horse there. Bred to be, anyway."

He had also swerved aside himself, avoiding giving his real opinion of Arcadia, at least, to an official who was a stranger to him. Jihan let the subject turn. "So I was told when I bought him."

"He looks like a Perry's Comet."

"That is his sire's name. –You have a good eye for horseflesh."

Windland shrugged again. "Size and set of his head and shoulders."

"Do the people of the Blue Grass really still regard Arcadia as 'the Fortress?'"

Windland merely nodded. They reached a turning and he took it, a lane between fields of hemp and corn, its packed earth shaded by spreading trees. Leaf-filtered light passed over his face, dimming the coppery burnish of his hair and blue of his feather. He frowned slightly. "Not much coming and going between Arcadia and the Blue, except business."

"Why should there not be? Maybe I'll race my horse."

"You'll be welcome at the meets. Careful, though. He's not made for mountain trails."

"I would have preferred grazing him today." Jihan glanced back at the riders. "No doubt he's not the only one who'd rather roam free. But I want a backup of a few skilled swords, not an invasion of the Provincial Guard."

Windland glanced back too. Jihan had been right—this leader had his riders' attention at once. He liked that. "Makes sense to us." Then he smiled. "Anyway, we consider we'll be envied in Gate City, Commander Jihan."

"From what I was told, you need no borrowed honor," Jihan returned the courtesy. "The caravan leader who has never lost cargo to the highwaymen."

"Me?" Windland grinned. "I'm not even respectable. Not here, anyway."

"Because you took to the roads, or because you serve the Domed City?"

"Both."

It was exactly that, his position between the two, this province and the Caverns, that made him the guide Jihan wanted, one who could see what he missed in the locals and translate him accurately to them.

"My clerks think we seek a dead man," he told the caravan leader. "They have two theories. Assessor Waldis died and someone wishes to keep his belongings. Or else a quarrel broke out and the Assessor was killed in the heat of it. What do you think?"

"I had a few dealings with Assessor Waldis. Not the heated quarrel type."

"One need not quarrel to be quarrelled with."

Windland nodded, acknowledging.

"Another idea occurred to me, though my clerks disagreed," Jihan told him. "If the villagers have little to lose, might they try to gain? To put it bluntly, do they think Arcadia so weak they might kidnap him?"

"That's war thinking."

"Conflict is not my intention," Jihan returned with sincere emphasis.

The lane plunged into a stand of woods, bearing sharply downward. He gave the bay more rein.

Windland speculated, "What if there's already trouble, but not between the villagers and us? You asked if I'd been to Tanglevine. Reason I've stayed away from there, it's got a bad name. People have disappeared there before."

"Oh?" Jihan glanced at him, startled. How like those fools in Arcadia not to know that. Or, just not to say so?

"They're rough in Woodhollow district, but hardworking, minding their own business. The odd thing is that they'd ask to be inspected at all."

The lane was dwindling to a mere trail, roots lacing it and branches meeting overhead. The daylight was reduced to flecks studding the dim green.

"They have something to hide, you mean? Waldis may have stumbled onto something he should not have?"

Windland shrugged. "Might be."

"Then as you say, why was he sent for? Feuding village factions?"

The leader nodded.

"A feud between whom?"

The caravan leader rode in silence for a while, but at last shook his head. "There I can't help you. Not till we know more. But my advice," he stopped himself. A guide was one thing. An assistant, another. It was a line most Domenes never allowed an Outlander to cross.

"Your advice is?"

Windland met his eyes for a moment. "While we're at Tanglevine, none of us should go anywhere alone. Especially you."

"Assessor Waldis worked alone."

Jihan saw that the ambiguity of his reply was not lost on the caravan leader. "Caution may be wise," he added, "but if caution profits us nothing, I make no promises to remain cautious." He grinned reassuringly. "If they expect another Waldis, they're in for a surprise."

The tree stands alone on the hill. Its branches spread like thoughts that go on and on. You could think over the whole countryside from here, maybe the whole world, swell and lull of long grass east to Redwing Creek, the road, Teasel's foaling barn.

South to where the willows dip and Shady Creek joins Redwing at Frogtown, where the bull-croakers and the peepers make their racket all night.

Rising above the willows like an island, the blackened hill where the Sun Circle was. The Domene soldiers smashed its stones, yet Uncle Tyree's voice still came from the grass, chanting at dawn, and fainter, Wisteria's ancient singing. We danced there, so the soldiers burnt even the grass.

Now only bitter tears come when it rains. But Fared's voice I can find nowhere. Fared with his dandelion hair has gone to the Sun.

Kia says that should make me happy.

Kia just accepts her grief. She's too old to know.

Over the rise westward, out of sight, the brick school the Domenes built. North, the sod roofs and green village circle of Upthegrove where Hemmie moved her kiln and tore down the wall, and my mama thinks I'll take over the shop, but how can I when the screaming echoes from every stone?

"Pay attention," Kia says gently. She nudges me and points at the limb overhead. A wasp nest hangs among the leaves. "Gonna stir 'em up. Gonna put it in their little bug heads it's Spinner bothered 'em."

"Don't!"

Spinner grazes down the hill, minding his own business. He's iron dark now, but a handsome dapple grey is what he'll be. So curious he'll push his nose over your shoulder to see anything you've got in your hands. His soft lips tickle your ear, and his breath is sweet as clover.

"Up to you to protect him."

"I've never managed it," I object. "There's way too many wasps, enough to make him sick."

Kia only closes her eyes. I clench my fingers tight as her lips shape silent words. A buzz rustles the leaves. And buzzes. And fuss, and fretting, and buzzing. They swarm around the nest, red ones spiraling out seeking, sleek angry wasps with their stingers cocked. Spinner flicks his tail, innocent. They sense that motion and head for him, a big red cloud of them.

"Kia!" But she only stands there with her eyes closed.

I make myself drop my arms to my sides, loose, hands open like she's taught me. There's a stirring in the ground. I've felt that before, but never when I needed it.

I spread my fingers, I feel it through my bare feet, I feel it move up through me, sap rising in a stem. Not my power, not of my making, but more me than the thoughts I hoarded so stubborn, or the fears that lift away like a white wing flashing in the sky. I'm held by my heels to the hillside but free, raising my arms into the far blue of the sky where one finger touches the Sun.

Wasps in confusion, I sing whatever comes into my head. Wasps slow down, tuck in your stingers, slow down, forget. Yawn, sleepy wasps. Remember home, fly back, fly back to your tree.

And they do!

Lazily they loop over Spinner's head, drift over, scout their limb, their leaves, their sticky white nest, find it untrespassed, find it comfy. Squeezing their wings to their hard, thin bodies they creep into the holes like something running backward into a colander. Spinner kicks out a back *leg, then settles back to grazing, not a sting on his hide.*

It's me who tingles. I did it! I protected him!

It's only wasps, but I've learned how, and I'll practice, and I'll work and my craft will grow. Even now, maybe I could send these wasps scooting over the hill, into the brick school to attack the Domene teacher.

Small minded, and I won't do it. Wasps won't drive 'em away. But it'd give the little'uns some joy, and they could use that. And they'd fear the teacher less if they saw her blundering and whirling and flapping her robes.

I throw back my head to laugh at the thought. Tears burn like acid down my face.

~ 5 ~

The Woods

he miles wound along a ridge over-looking a rumpled country of treetops that creased where the folds of streams gathered, then mounted higher into the distance. All was covered with forest except where stone cropped out, offering naked edges to the sky.

Descending, the trail struck a shadowy creek that fell over rims of grey or yellowish rock with hesitant notes, deep and gurgling. Flies buzzed in the closeness, making his horse swish its tail irritably.

The wet weather had coaxed the woodland into strange burgeonings. Spotted snails oozed up a tree beneath leaves broad enough to do credit to a jungle. Thick moss furred the ground. Unseen birds squabbled in the humid shadows. Beyond the crowding obscurity of the leaves Jihan glimpsed an inviting brightness, perhaps an open glade. He considered letting the bay gallop there to relieve it of the flies' pestering.

"Careful to your left," said the scrawny rider behind him. The world shifted, or his vision did. His stomach followed it. The green between the trunks was too bright. His eye caught a small ripple far below. What he had taken for a meadow was water in a sunlit ravine.

They halted for a meal of bread, fruit and a surprisingly tasty local cheese, buttery with a savor of roasted nuts.

Jihan rested on the moss beneath a tree. The dark-skinned rider, Tal, napped on the dry pine needles, the woman Camellia with her head on his chest. Arn, the scrawny one, went down to wade in the stream, and grey haired Daw disappeared between the trees.

The leader showed no more concern at their scattering than they did at wandering off without permission. Windland had put down grain for the horses and now moved among them, sliding a hand down slender, steely legs, picking up hooves, feeling muscular bodies for sore spots. Flecks of brightness swam over the scarred toe of a boot, washed a tanned forearm, caught the jewel blue of the jay feather. Sometimes the shadows obscured him entirely until a movement revealed him, not behind the

horses as Jihan had thought, but unsnagging a
burr from a mane, or leaning against a tree
watching Arn splash naked in the stream below.

What had a Domene woman to do with
such an elemental, Jihan wondered idly as he
fought off sleep. Had her friends ceased to know
her when she matched so far beneath herself?

Probably. The caravanner's audacity was
commendable, but the marriage would close
more doors to the woman than they opened to
him.

Possibly it was a rash choice she now
regretted, but Jihan thought she might have
recognized possibilities in this Outlander. Maybe
he had already found one provincial with
ability—and just as valuable, with ambition.

Jihan leaned back against the tree trunk.
The metallic drone of insects rose from the
surrounding branches, spreading like ripples in a
pond until the woods beyond the stream rang
with it, and the ridge above, thousands by the
sound. The woman rider's head stirred on her
man's chest, and the horses crunched their feed.
Windland sang to the whirring drone.

"To the dim places and the tangle vine places
Where leaves drown in pools of green,
Where trees, beyond trees, beyond trees,

Beyond trees
Watch your steps to cover them over,
Cover you over—"

"Appropriate," Jihan remarked. "But not very heartening."

When the caravanner did not continue, Jihan pulled a stick from between the roots. "Does the song have more verses?"

Picking his way through the trees like a stag, Windland came and hunkered down. "It's not a song, the words just came to me."

"Why does this village make you so uneasy?"

"Like I said, Tanglevine's got a bad name. In old times, there was plague. It was a century ago, but it's a terrible memory around this district."

"You have not said all that you know."

Windland's eyes mirrored the leaves. The insects pulsed. "Some say Tanglevine is cursed."

Jihan broke the twig with a snap. "Its inconvenient remoteness is a curse."

The caravan leader merely watched him. Unseen birds rustled. They both glanced up, but the foliage hung too heavily to make out any of the small nameless things ticking among the vines. "These woods could not help but breed superstitions," Jihan conceded.

"The villagers believe in the curse. It might shape what they do."

Picking up another stick, Jihan began peeling it. "Well, then. Tell me what they believe."

"That it causes storms, floods that roar down before you can blink—that happens all over the mountains, but they say Lost Creek leaves its bed and rages wherever it wants like a black dragon with ridges on its back, pieces of trees and whatever else it's gouged up, that it uses to drown people and animals, even slam holes in buildings."

"On purpose? My elder son scares his little brother with such tales."

The caravanner did not smile.

"Do you believe in this curse?" Jihan asked him.

The insects rasped like long inhalations. At last Windland shrugged. "Hardly matters, does it? There's a job of work to do." He stood and gave a low whistle.

The two napping riders started awake. Splashes came from below as Arn left the water. Windland went to the horses, but Jihan remained where he was. The caravanner was right. If the villagers feared this curse, it had a kind of power, and that bore remembering.

Jihan prodded the earth with his stick. The more he learned, the less he liked the prospect before them, either. He was glad he had not entrusted this touchy business to some inept tax inspector. Breaking the stick in half he aimed each piece at a slender tree up the hillside. One satisfying rap echoed, then another. The insects went silent for a few breaths.

Arn led his mount over. "Leg up, Ward?"

"No need." Taking the reins, Jihan sprang lightly into the saddle.

The rider's eyes flicked to Windland. The leader made no sign, but Arn gave a cheeky grin. His straw colored hair was still damp.

Jihan rode to Windland. "We will say we have come to resume the inspections." The horses stepped into the narrow green tunnel of the trail. "If they tell us the Assessor left the village, I will have two riders scour the roads again, though I doubt they'll find anything. We will look for signs of the Assessor in the village, of course, but we'll also watch the villagers. My real hope is to find informants. If there is a feud, their enmities may help us."

Windland nodded once in acknowledgment, then rode in silence.

Trunks and limbs slanted at confused angles, fading in every direction to half-guessed dimness. Stones tilted among the trees as if disordered by some upheaval. Amid the snarl of saplings and man-high ferns they looked like a gigantic ruined highway. Jihan disliked the sight. Something's wings grazed his cheek and he started.

Ahead, Windland appeared and disappeared in shadows and sun flecks as if he neared some border between waking and dreams. Green light rippled over Jihan's own hands and his horse's neck like rills in a stream so that to himself he seemed to waver on the verge of nature's chaos.

What was this strange lethargy that seeped like an insinuating dream, slowly infecting the eyes with bewilderment and the mind with dizziness?

A thick hump of root became visible to him only as the bay stepped over it. A large tree fed from it, bark gaping on a hollow as black as any cavern seam. What mad impulse urged him to plunge into it, what seduction tempted him to escape into the depths of those mysterious thickets, or to lose himself beyond recall in the streak of sunlight trembling along the veins of a leaf?

Jihan shook off the sleep that had nearly claimed him in the saddle. "How these trees obstruct sight," he remarked wryly. "Let us hope the village is in a clearing."

From the dimness ahead came Windland's disembodied voice. "It's not."

Then, a few old houses of weathered wood. A piddly jumble against the hillside, not painted, no glass in the windows, only plank shutters shoved open. Blacksmith's, store like a shed, next to that, the stay. Doors wide to the breeze, people inside at their afternoon did-do's, making or cooking or canning for the cold months.

Pine and oak climb above the crookedy no-count bottomland where sassafras nudges paw paw trees. What to do with such a place? Let the buzzards peck it up and shit it out, my man used to say.

But I wouldn't go back to the Sun's places, the willow places and pasture places. Not as long as I could hear the screams and see the deaths I saw there. That means never.

Bells tinkle. People swoop to their doorways as the caravan comes up the trail, trotting purposeful, with—oh ho—two at its head! One's a right splendor with that long dark hair and embroidered sash gleaming over a fine crimson shirt. And a strong body under that. The Domene.

Mountains lean, clouds tumble over and over, the whole world slides toward Lost Creek.

No unwishing it now. Can't he feel what he stirs up just by coming here? What he tempts?

But no, look at the presumptuous thing, riding like a one-man army, so proud in the saddle, heels of his polished boots down, head high.

Way too handsome. Strength balances with grace in his face, in the quick arch of his brows, and each eye a rattlesnake! That no nonsense beard nearly hides lips only a man would think to hide, sensuous.

How many's come to grief from him? He glances over our little village like he owns it.

Who's he think he is? And these diseased old woods, can they hold the turmoil he provokes in them?

What about the other? From my dream, only he's clearer now. Long legged red mare pauses as he tenses. He doesn't show it, just takes a quick breath over his left shoulder, spits to his right. Then he looks at Tanglevine again. Ha. I can hear his heart beating. Got a faded shirt and scuffed boots, hole in the thigh of his britches, hair the color of turning sycamore leaves.

Never saw him before, but he's familiar as the call of a redwing. No idea who he is, but he's one of us.

What's he want here, and with a Domene?

The rest, what you'd expect. Riders from hither and yon in their feathers and luck charms, sturdy geldings and mares sure footed but no candle to that bay or even the leader's part-thoroughbred.

Then I see.

I know why the caravanner from the Blue Grass is here. What we might do if I dare to hope, if he's strong enough. If the Domene, if, if only the Domene.

People watch them ride to the stay, though nobody goes out. Only Diddie, to welcome and see if they're hungry. She hollers up her two sons to help. Every eye's on the Domene. Not a one but knows why he's here. What he hopes to find. How deep he's in beyond his reckoning.

It all depends on the Domene.

~ 6 ~

The Inn

indland pointed between the trees. "That looks like the stay. Inn, you'd call it. I'll get us rooms." He turned to the riders. "Take your time with the horses. Be friendly, share our brandy, and keep your eyes and ears open."

A woman came out to the inn porch. She called a welcome, then leaned over the rail shouting two names. Two gawky boys in their teens came to help with the horses, her sons or grandsons. She looked anywhere between thirty-five and sixty, her hair as faded as her shirt and trousers.

Letting Windland handle the arrangements, Jihan fixed the layout of the village in his mind. Seemingly, its traffic went mostly on foot. A mere path straggled between the inn, smithy and houses. Another followed the bank of the creek.

Upstream it disappeared into the green gloom of the forest. Woodland birds called. The patches of light had the slant of mid-afternoon at most. The caravan leader had done well.

He handed the bay's reins to Arn and climbed the weathered steps to the porch, past split rail chairs shaded by vines, into a square public room.

Four thick posts supported its low ceiling, with a staircase at the back corner. The wooden walls had never seen paint or whitewash. Windows stood open to the leafy shade, but the room was hot. Judging from a pot dangling over a burning fire, the hearth also served as the inn's kitchen. A plank on a trestle made a counter. Windland rested an elbow on it, chatting with the innkeeper as she took clay mugs from the shelves and stooped to fill them at a barrel. The only others in the room were two young women whispering between themselves at the other end of the counter.

"Rooms are easy. Have all three if you want," the innkeeper was saying. "Food, that's different. My brother's mule, she been hire to the farms along Tanglevine Creek, been keep me in meat and extries, you know?"

She plunked a mug on the plank and began filling another. "When the storm come she's up in Shon's pasture, took shelter in the barn. Wind blew it in and squashed her flat, bless her ol' heart." She put the other mug before the caravanner. "So. Nothin' from her and no paying guests—only that tax man, and he didn't stay as long as he promised. You can share what I've got, stew and cornbread. I put two squirrels in it, enough to flavor it a little."

She shot a dubious glance in Jihan's direction and lowered her voice. "Think a Domene can stomach squirrel stew?"

"Bet he's ate worse," Windland answered.

Hardly courteous, for all that the pot reeked of wild onions. Jihan turned to compliment its smell and saw the innkeeper return the caravanner's grin. Some backhanded praise had been given, he supposed, or amusement at a Domene eating rodents—or worse. Jihan did not care which, so long as the locals accepted the caravanner as more or less one of themselves.

He took a seat at the nearer of the two long tables, where he could watch the room's occupants as well as the yard and porch. The pair of women by the trestle glanced sideways at him. They were young, in their teens, and the blouses of both revealed too much shoulder and breast. One tried to catch his eye. When he ignored her they giggled.

Windland brought the beer. Stepping over the long bench he sat and unbuttoned his shirt, letting it flap over his tanned chest. "Hot in here," he excused himself, though Jihan doubted the niceties of table manners counted for much in such a place.

"Did the Assessor settle with you before he left?" Jihan asked casually.

The innkeeper began wiping the counter with a damp cloth. "He stayed two days, paid for two days." The rag slurped vigorously over the plank, betraying her. As did the poor stew. He doubted she had gotten any money from Waldis.

"What of his meals and fodder? If he left any unpaid balance I will settle it now."

Her calloused hand closed on the rag. But she resumed wiping. "He didn't run out, he settled up as he should." Tossing the cloth into a bucket she crossed the room to stir the pot. Windland swallowed some of the beer and met Jihan's eye at the watered-down taste.

"So, sounds like your Assessor still didn't turn up?" the innkeeper inquired, bending over the fire with her back to them.

"No."

"Right sorry to hear it." She shook her head. "Got some naisty drops along these roads. Mudslides too, with all this rain."

"Yes, I can well believe that. Did he say where he meant to go, or why?"

She shook her head and pinched some salt into the stew.

"What occurred that might account for his leaving the inspections unfinished?"

"Nothin' I know of."

"Even the smallest detail you can recall may prove helpful."

She straightened, scratching her arm thoughtfully. "Well. You might say he acted kind of skittish."

The riders came onto the porch, boots thumping the boards. Determined not to lose the opening, Jihan raised his voice above them. "Skittish? How so?"

Arn looked in, met Windland's glance and nodded as if spoken to. He gave Tal a shove on the shoulder and the riders settled on the porch.

Jihan watched the innkeeper cross to the counter, her cheeks and forehead flushed from the fire. Without facing him she turned to take more mugs from the shelves. "What did he do?" Jihan persisted.

She shrugged. "Talked about baid dreams."

Jihan glanced at Windland, who silently mouthed *bad*. Jihan tried for something more useful. "Who served him as guide?"

Her shoulders stiffened. Windland sucked his cheeks slightly. She bent to draw the riders' beer. "Served him? That clerk, he been serve him. Some of the farmers showed him the roads, bein' neighborly." Gripping the mugs by all four handles, she took the beer out to the riders.

Silently Jihan cursed her quibbling over an unimportant word. He must remember not to use it. Blue Grass provincials were not the only Outlanders who turned the worthy notion of service to the Domed City inside out, failing to understand that even the Council Master served.

The girls at the counter tittered harshly. As if wakened by the sound, the insects outside began a loud rasping. It rose to fill the humid afternoon, echoing from the sides of the narrow valley.

And black spring leaves brushed my cheeks, tender and velvet and fragile as moths' wings. Moths' wings crowding to fill the night. And the sound of them spreading on for miles. They say the sea sighs so. The hissing, and the thunder beneath. I'm lost in the endless waves of the hills, and glad to be.

I raise a hand. Part my fingers. Let the blue flicker along them, showing the path. The tree trunks twist and gnarl, gleaming dim as silver in an old, forgotten treasure chest.

An elusive spice fills the night, some wildflower I have never seen. I imagine it wonderful, petals pale as the moon, softly furred like a peach, opening among the ferns. I breathe in the peace of the world not shaped by people or deformed by war, a harmony beyond the mind's understanding, but felt in the core of the soul.

Could be the Domenes never came this far. Could be not a one has poked a feeler into this corner that the world's forgot it has. That's not promised, but I can hope.

Oh, and the hopes a woman can hold onto, despite all.

Peace. To gaze at the constellations at midnight or take the morning wash to the creek without always looking fast over her shoulder. Dancing and good talk and laughter and using the arts she's gained to help her neighbors. Neighbors whose faces the Domene torches never burned into the memory of the world's night.

Such delights I picture to myself, even in these times.

A creek gurgles, keeping me company as it runs by my side. I sing along with it, do a slow turn and sway, raise my arms like the trees', nobody spying me but the whipoorwills.

Then through the lace of the vines, light. A candle in a window. Another. And a lantern hanging in a porch. A stay. I lift my hand higher, let the blue illumination flow through me till it's good and bright. The tree roots cast blue shadows. The undersides of the leaves glisten.

Faces show at the windows, not fearing, just curious. It's a hopeful sign. Unlikely that soldiers come knocking here. Here, their little'uns still run far and wide, and nobody bothers their old people. As I near the stay a woman leans over the porch rail. "Welcome, mother," she calls. She's older than me, but she knows what I am. "Needin' a place to sleep? I got good beds and turkey pie. Tanglevine's got no healer and Moon Lissa's old granddaddy been sick."

Her voice is hopeful. "Are you a healer?"

One of the girls poked the other. "You smell somethin'?"

"What?"

"Somethin' naisty. Like the insides of a cave."

They were staring at him. The taller was slender with fair hair that might have been attractive had she washed it. The other was rather stunted, with bad skin. She answered her friend with a shrug and went around the trestle to refill her mug at the innkeeper's barrel.

"I'll have the innkeeper ask all who wish inspections to gather here tonight," Jihan told Windland quietly. "We'll reconstruct the Assessor's schedule and see what each farmer has to say. Our inspections will retrace his steps as far as possible. Two of your riders can accompany us."

"Got muscles and a tan, though," mused the smaller girl. "Didn't know they made 'em pretty. Domenes, I mean."

Windland ignored her. "Any two. My riders are all good trackers."

"I do love green eyes," the girl persisted.

"Ain't green," her friend answered. "Dirt-colored and mean."

"Green. Dark, like a shady place."

"You can have 'im. Give me the saddlehopper."

Blue Grass womanhood in all its glory. Brazen, frivolous and no doubt as cheap as it came.

Windland turned on the bench. "Leave be. The Master of Revenues is here to help."

"What do I care?" the frowzy headed one snarled. "I got no land or cow to my name."

"Then show respect for those that do," snapped the innkeeper, coming through the door. "Flibbertygibbets. Hey, you been at my beer again?"

The shorter girl let the tip of her tongue peep out.

The innkeeper looked over. "You want these no-counts gone?"

Windland shook his head. He turned that blue gaze of his on the girls. Their giggling paused. He beckoned.

They exchanged a smirk.

Jihan frowned, but the caravanner did not see him. "C'mere," he cajoled, as if they were two fillies he had a mind to tame. "Got something to show you."

"Can that not wait?" Jihan growled in rising irritation. Were *none* of these people any better than the mares and studs they kept?

The flibbertygibbets crept nearer, arms around each other and snickering. Giving Jihan a wide berth, they lit on either side of the caravanner. "Hey pretty," one murmured.

The corners of Windland's mouth indented in the hint of a smile and he leaned back on the bench, his open shirt sliding apart to reveal smooth brown skin over angular muscles, a small pink nipple, a bloom of color. Rippling over his left waist and upper hip, a tattooed heron waded in a swirl of water.

The two flinched as if he had hit them.

Casually, Windland turned up his mug, finishing his beer.

"Hunh!" the taller one stuck out her chin like a sulky child. Deliberately she leaned down, stroking the bird's curved neck with her forefinger. "And if I tickle it, what'll that cause?" But she was just saving face. She straightened and stalked away, the other in her wake.

Windland drew his shirt together. From the counter, the innkeeper considered him silently.

"What does the tattoo mean?" Jihan asked quietly.

"A heron," Windland answered, buttoning. "They live all up and down the Blue Grass creeks."

"They fear it."

"They don't. It's—" he turned to the innkeeper. "What would you call it, a clan sign?"

She nodded, but the girls sidled out the door.

If they did not fear the tattoo, they feared his clan.

"You have overstepped," Jihan told him.

Windland sighed. "With respect, Ward Jihan, I didn't ask you because I didn't expect you to understand."

"Try."

"You heard 'em. We were outsiders. Fair game. Others might have more manners, but they'd feel the same. Now I have a village and family. Maybe even cousins here. So do you, while you're with me." His voice dropped below the innkeeper's hearing. "Now, whatever happens, they're accountable."

"To Arcadia, as are you." Jihan returned quietly. "It is you who fail to understand. We were neutral. For the right price we could have dealt with anyone. Now, whatever is going on, you have involved us. We have now inherited enmities and embroilments that you have already admitted you do not understand."

"Maybe, but on the side against killing."

"I have only your word for that." Jihan stepped over the bench, told the innkeeper to spread news of the evening's gathering, and ordered bath water brought to his room.

~ 7 ~

The Gathering

cold wind seethes through the valley, rattling the bare branches' knuckles. The bleak of the sky says snow. The timbers of Tanglevine creak, plank against plank, joint against peg, the smoke streaming from the chimneys fast sideways.

Some that have endured the cutting chill to hunt traipse down from the hills. A stag to divvy, the smell of fires and tight shutters promising snug comfort, the last nip from the flask tingling in tired legs. A little laughter. A little song.

Hooves on the frozen trail. Clank of bridles and gear. The song halts, only the wind kreeling on high and thin. People watch as riders appear between the grey trunks and stony ground, trotting purposeful with a robed man at their head.

His long black hair gusts in the chill. It's put color in his cheeks but he's a Domene. The end of his grey sash whips, and he carries the silver headed staff of a tax collector. He's so thin you'd think the slightest fit of wind would carry him off, but it doesn't. He sits his horse firm. Behind him, a detachment of Provincial Guard, claptrap of swords and truncheons clattering against their saddles.

The stripped finger-bones of the trees can't catch or hold the noise, it slips through them to run along the hillsides. The stones send it shuddering back.

The Domene halts in front of Diddie's stay. The Guard halt behind him. He surveys the houses, the workshops and animal sheds, the hunters. In his weasel-bright, weasel-black eyes, no flicker, not even scorn. He speaks no greeting. The hunters draw closer together. The gaunt fingers of the wind probe. Their thin nails pierce our flesh.

Arn wandered in from the porch, wiping the sweat of the humid night. He took the pipe Daw offered him and strolled to Windland. "Big bunch of everybody's in the yard."

That news needed no bearer. The sound of voices rose through the open door louder than the night crickets, and shapes moved in the twilight below. Jihan eked out his meal with the last of the cheese they had brought with them, soft now and pungent, but necessary. Everything about the stew had proved meager except the wild onions.

Windland took the pipe Arn proffered and drew. Jihan smelled the resinous scent of hemp. "Hope they don't all want inspections."

"They don't talk like." Arn took back the pipe. "There's grampaws, babies, Aunt Loolabell's third cousins. We're the only fun in town."

Windland shrugged. "Good. Let's see who-all Tanglevine's got."

"Let 'em in now?"

Jihan finished his cheese and motioned the innkeeper to clear away the crockery. "Yes, send them." When the rider was out of earshot he turned to the caravan leader. "Watch the villagers closely. Advise me. But remember that on this expedition you are not independent."

Windland pulled the paper, pen and ink bottle to him.

That was not an answer. "Consider it an order."

The innkeeper set a lamp on the table. Villagers were straggling in, many bringing tobacco or hemp pipes into the already smoky room. Most held mugs. The innkeeper's sons had done a brisk trade in the yard. Men and women of every age milled in the stuffy heat. All had a pinched look, even the children who dashed among the adults' legs with all the noisy undiscipline of Outlander young. Here, such joy was probably all too short-lived. The adults were gaunt with habitual worry and illness. Sallow skin, coughs, and bad teeth were common. Jihan saw some misshapen limbs and a distorted spine.

The villagers' glances at him ranged from dubious curiosity to outright hostility. Clearly, the innkeeper's courtesy was merely professional and Tanglevine thought an official from Arcadia as likely to bring trouble as relieve it.

And so he might. That would depend on what he found.

He and the caravan leader established themselves in the middle of the table, facing the room. At his word, Windland organized the villagers. They moved back readily, allowing those with claims to gather before the table.

They seemed to understand the caravanner with ease, and he them, though in the din of voices Jihan had trouble following their speech. It was faster than the caravanner's, the harsh R and nasal vowels savoring more of the

Mountains than the Blue Grass to his ear. But the names they gave were Blue Grass, mostly after flora, fauna and forces of nature. They used no patronymics, but had surnames made by tacking an S onto the end of some ancestor's name. Jihan hid his amusement as the caravanner introduced him as "J'han Edwarns"— a fine rustic name for Mirabil to tease him with.

Windland occasionally translating, he informed the farmers that tax relief depended on his inspection of all storm damages, including those already viewed by Assessor Waldis.

"Unfortunately, not even the Assessor's horse has turned up. Presumably the paperwork was in his saddlebag." That drew no comment. Interesting. Hadlin had reported questioning some of them about the saddle he'd glimpsed, yet he saw not so much as a flicker of unease.

To his surprise, it was his instruction to draw a map of Tanglevine that touched a nerve. A few of them muttered, but no one stepped forward to take the pen Windland offered.

"Surely Assessor Waldis asked for a map?"

"We showed him the way," contradicted a woman from the back.

"Who did?"

"Whoever's next for inspection. We'll do the same for you."

"A map'd just get you good an' lost," added another. "Right many forking trails up in the hills, apt to get yourself turned around in the woods."

"All the same, I want one."

Closed faces merely watched him. Jihan frowned at the caravan leader. Windland let his pen drop, displaying open palms. "Just the farms you want inspected," he reasoned with them. "Roads to take, landmarks to find our way, Tanglevine Creek—we don't need every gully and snake hole."

Glances among them. At last two moved forward. Jihan silently watched Windland seat them at a corner of the table with pen and paper. Locals sometimes hid certain places from officials, valleys used for illegal crops, mines operating without City permission and the like.

But if it was a black market operation they wanted to conceal, it was no lucrative one from the look of them. He was very curious to see which areas they left blank.

"As for Assessor Waldis," Jihan continued, "after eight days I see little hope he still lives, but I will not give up until I discover his fate. I will search the roads again, but you were the last to speak with him. The more you can tell me of what he did and said, the sooner I can leave you in peace, return to Arcadia and satisfy the Governor."

"That'n come an ais' those questions already," said a stocky woman with thick black brows. "We been tell all we know."

"The Clerk of Revenues Hadlin? Yes, he has reported to me. I am here to learn more." Jihan leaned forward. "Let us begin with the inspections. Which did Assessor Waldis complete?"

The black-browed woman glanced into a corner. Several men and women leaned there. None returned her glance.

"He looked at my spring and barn," a woman in a headscarf answered. As she marked her damaged property on the map, Jihan noticed a lizard tattooed on her hand.

Others followed, the woman's brother, one Moon Lissas with drowned livestock, one Song Becks. "Flood wiped out my chicken coop and soaked the food stored in my cellar." She circled a spot in the hills.

Jihan consulted the map. It showed only the creek running east to west, a circle for the village, hills on either side, and the lines of roads leading to farms here and there. Her mark seemed a mile or more from Tanglevine Creek. "There is another stream?"

Song Becks faced him fiercely. "Not on my land there ain't." The gathering watched in silence. In hostility. Not at an undeserving claim. At him. For the first time Jihan felt a familiar prickle in his back. Alertness. Danger. The exhilarating sharpening of his senses at the possibility of violence. But why? What mattered to them so much that all of them wanted to conceal it? Even the innkeeper had stopped drawing beer to listen.

Challenge accepted, Jihan thought. Whatever your secret, I will discover it. He motioned the caravan leader to list Song Becks' farm. "The Assessor completed your inspection?"

The silence was absolute. "'Bout twilight," Song Becks answered.

Jihan waited for more. Her glance over her shoulder was brief, but it was at the same corner, at the sullen bunch that refused to speak or acknowledge.

"Don't they look cut from the same cloth?" Windland whispered. They did. Dark hair, coarse features, heavy brows.

Jihan prompted quietly, "And then?"

The tension in the room was thicker than the smoke. In the back a child put up a wail. Song Becks shrugged. "My husband brought him back here to the stay. Just ais' Diddie, she'll tell you."

Jihan studied the woman for a long moment, letting the tension mount. The child's crying rose to an earsplitting howl. As people looked toward the noise, Song Becks stepped back into the gathering. The opportunity slipped away. Jihan let it go—for now.

An old man took her place. "My turn been next. Owl's my name. Had a fire, wind blew over a lamp in my house."

A woman elbowed through, followed by a man who gripped her arm. Freeing it, the woman drew herself up. "I'm Lily Becks. My daughter Marcy didn't say so before, but the storm blew a huge elm down bang on her shed. Roof's in pieces. That's where she been store her pig's corn, and with this rain—"

"Master Revenues, that land's my daughter's," the man contradicted. "I give it her."

Lily turned on her husband. "It's hers, but she's not of age. Even if she was—"

"She don't want it inspected, she been told you. Where's Marcy, you all? Find and ais' her." He shrugged apologetically at Jihan. "Marcy's grabbed onto some notion, I ain't sayin' it's real, but to her it is, you understand?"

"Here she is," someone called. A round faced girl came down the stairs and the crowd parted to let her through. The child that had been tormenting their eardrums suddenly hushed.

The girl's brown hair frizzed in thick curls and her eyes had a wide expression like the caravanner's did in fleeting moments, but her vacancy did not change as the villagers steered her to her parents.

"You see how she is, Master. –Where were you?" her mother demanded.

Marcy stared at Jihan and Windland, refusing to speak.

Her father sighed. "Like my wife says, you see how she is."

The child wormed his way through the gathering. With a cry the girl caught him up as if she imagined Domenes were cannibals. "Don't want nobody around me an' Poke."

"They won't come near you, they just want to see the shed roof."

"No!"

"Leave her be, we'll get by."

Jihan restrained an exasperated movement. If Waldis had not gone there the storm could carry away shed, girl and howling brat, for all he cared. Maybe the girl could not help herself, but such a public display between man and wife was disgraceful. If they could not rule themselves, the law must rule them. "Your daughter is not yet of age, you say."

"Not for four months and two days," her mother confirmed.

"As her father has said—" Something nudged his foot. Windland's boot. The caravanner angled his papers. He had scribbled, *Mother gardian. Father only if mother incompitent.*

Jihan changed course in mid-sentence, "—he gave her the land. It is no longer his. Permission rests with you." He motioned the woman to take the pen. The villagers watched without surprise as Lily made her mark. Even the father only patted the girl's shoulder, saying she and the child could spend the inspection day at her parents' house. Whatever the girl's qualms, Jihan's decision clearly had the gathering's approval. He called the old man Owl forward again.

~ 8 ~

The Witch

inally it was over. Twelve farms to inspect, all told. A few of the villagers stayed on to sip beer but were not talking much. The shuffling and dealing sounds of the riders' card game came from the porch.

Jihan had Diddie the innkeeper refill Windland's mug and his own. The more he considered the blunder the caravanner had spared him, the larger he realized it would have been.

It was not just the insult he would have offered to the village woman's intelligence— though the mother of such a daughter might keenly resent that. It was the suspicion he would have provoked about his own intentions. He would have been putting his own authority above Domene law.

At least, Domene law as it existed in this province. It was difficult keeping track of the provincial variations, concessions to differing local customs. He was familiarizing himself with Blue Grass law, but had not encountered guardianship. It made sense, considering the questionability of paternal rights where paternity itself was often uncertain. The girl Marcy was a mother, for instance, with no husband in evidence.

"Had you not stopped me, the women of the village might even now have us bound hand and foot in poison ivy," he acknowledged his debt.

"Mmm, naked?" The corners of Windland's mouth indented. "Wonder what they'd do to us then."

"An hour's pleasure in exchange for a week's torment?" Jihan smiled. "Is it really worth it?"

Windland shrugged. "Poison ivy don't blister me."

How predictable. "It wouldn't."

The caravanner yawned and stretched his legs beneath the table. "Comes of growing up among it."

Jihan sipped the thin beer. "The women of your province fend for themselves like men. Are their freedoms really better than the protections Domene women enjoy? What says your wife?"

"Simura's a Master of Learning, she doesn't crave a road tramp telling her what to do."

"A special case. Then, it's her own choice not to ride caravan?"

Windland fought another yawn. "She did for a few years. Got tired of it."

"I don't wonder. From the Alabaster Halls to this?" He gestured at the bare room. "That she stuck it out for that long is admirable. Your wife sounds a remarkable woman."

"You're a Ward. Big house in one of those private chambers? Dozens of rooms, fountains, your own formations?"

"Something of that sort."

"Yet you didn't choose ease."

"No. But is it the same for a woman?" Jihan frowned, trying to imagine Mirabil here, or as a fighter on the frontier. He could not. Did she secretly long for such a life? "I only know I'm glad my wife is safe from barbarians' arrows and woodlanders' knives." Jihan swirled the beer in his mug. "If it must be admitted, I also value knowing that Edwarn and Travertin are my sons."

"I'm my father's son," Windland returned amicably. "Just sired by a neighbor." He returned Jihan's startlement with a wink. Fact, or joke?

Best not to pursue it.

An owl's lament shivers from the highest branches, the little, ghostly kind, wailing soft and faint, wailing untelling regret. Through the secret dark of the woods the scent of sassafras breathes, and the carrion sweetness of the crimson petalled trillium. The song of the night bugs pulses, multitudinous voices each with a separate warning, like fate.

"Like destiny," mutters the old woman, poking her head and a shaft of light into the thick swirling night. The door opens more and now the amber is cat's eye yellow, green around its edges. And now she blows it out.

But her steps pad in the shadows, sure along the curvings of the root laced path. She talks to me sometimes, but now she's silent as death. She carries death with her. Like a pack on a tinker's back. Like a sack that when it's put down has lumps that shift, that keep crawling, furtive, hinting at no shape you want to see. Like a sack you'd give all you've got if she wouldn't open it. Only, the sack itself is death, famished maw, black trap, carried on a witch's back.

But if it is, what stirs inside it?

She comes into the lantern light, an old woman by herself, no pack on her back, only a long grey braid that swings like a snake.

And I swing, hiding from the eyes of the fish in the creek. I see the shadows crawl with no breezes. I hear the echo of a rock rolling down the hill. I feel it out there, watchful, waiting. But not patiently. Its malignant craving throbs deafening in the night.

The old woman puts a knobby hand on the rail. She climbs the steps of the stay, toting her invisible sack.

Jihan lowered his voice. "Did you notice the oddity? Two days of inspection and only three farms completed."

"'Eah," Windland murmured. "That Song Becks that got the last inspection, she went off with the bear-lookin' bunch. The ones with the eyebrows."

"Did she?"

Windland drew the lamp closer and went over the map and list. "They're Coves. Live up here." He pointed to farms marked in the hills north of the creek. Song's was close by.

"Let us learn more about these Coves."

An old woman rounded the table toward them. Jihan silenced. She stopped before them, putting her beer mug on the table. Sinews showed in her thin, sun burnt arms. Crescents darkened the lined skin under her eyes, but their grey irises glinted like pins. Wiry hair escaped a braid, sticking out at peculiar angles. "Well," she said.

"Good evening." Jihan felt his store of courtesy running low. He wanted sleep.

"Still ain't found your tax man, that it?" She smiled grimly. "What's that you said? 'I won't give up till I discover his fate?' Guess it's no good warning you to get out of here."

Sleep retreated. "None," Jihan answered. "Unless you can tell me what I need to know."

She snorted. "Not the way you mean."

"Then what can you tell us, Mother?" Windland asked quietly. Beneath the table where she could not see it his forefinger touched his thumb, making a circle. He kept them that way.

"I ain't your mama." Her eyes caught the red gleam of the fire's embers.

Windland gave her his blue gaze. "But you know more than us," he coaxed.

"And I'm too old to charm." On the side away from Windland her forefinger and thumb met, making the same circle he was making.

They faced one another in challenge, neither aware of the other's sign. "What's it to you, saddlehopper from Upthegrove?"

His fingers opened first. "You know why I'm here. I work for the Domed City."

She made a derisive noise.

He ignored it. "You think the Master of Revenues should know something or you wouldn't be here."

"By the sound of tonight, your Master of Revenues should know hoarders' heaps more than he does. If he had half the sense of his horse he'd gallop on out of here."

"As Assessor Waldis did after you warned him?" Jihan asked.

"As Assessor Waldis didn't, and you know it." She opened her forefinger and thumb. "I'm Sky Deers Wisteri. I'm the witch around Tanglevine, like my mama and grandmama before me. You'll find no other you can trust to scry you a creek, lay you cards or make you a charm against the plague. Want my help? Or not?"

"We might," Jihan answered. "Though we can do without the sorcerous trappings. Exactly what information do you offer, and at what fee?"

"You think I know *exactly* what happened to your tax man, or *exactly* where they've chucked his bones?"

"I'll settle for who *they* are."

"Listen, Revenues—or whatever your battle prizes called you when you hacked up their daddies and then poked your other weapon into them—"

Jihan started.

"—I don't know about witches in the Caverns, but witches of the Wisteria family vow ourselves as healers. We don't kill and we don't aid murderers. What I *can* do is help you find out who bushwhacked your tax man. Take it or leave it."

"There are no witches in the Caverns," Jihan informed her. "We have educated doctors and much less disease and suffering than people in the Outlands. We also have a willingness to share that condition that will make witches as obsolete in the Outlands as they are in the Domed City. If you have real information, we can deal. Otherwise, it has been a long day."

She turned from him. "This bumptious pup mistakes polish for graciousness and bullying for brains. If he don't mind his manners I'll let him dash headlong to perdition," she told Windland. "You want me, you look for me." Thumping her mug on the table she marched out.

Jihan let out a breath. "What a stalk of rhubarb."

"Got bite," Windland agreed, glancing at the doorway. But she was gone. Only the riders' voices came from the darkness, and the rhythm of the crickets.

"Well, she fails to amuse. She presumes too much on her age."

"Or her sight."

"Oh, come. You don't believe she has special powers?"

Windland shrugged.

Jihan frowned at the scarred table top. "It was only a guess," he fended off the edge of shame. "She must have heard I fought in the North. Not even a correct guess. Prize, not prizes. I fell to that temptation only once. A chieftain killed the girl's father, not I, and I did not force her. She considered it my right."

"It's their way, and you were far from home. But it bothers you."

Jihan met his eyes. "I'm a married man. I kept her for a month before I found her a husband. It was not right."

"What I mean is, you feel it. The witch caught a whiff. That's how they do. Same might work for the moods running around here. She might sense things we can't."

"With the same dubious accuracy? Such flickerings of the mind have no substance. The

Coves and Waldis' last inspection do. As for what you were doing with your hand—" Jihan joined his forefinger and thumb, "—a charm to ward off evil?"

"To make sure she's who she says."

"Did you know she was making the same sign against you?"

Windland grinned. "Was she?"

"Neither of you strikes much demonic terror in my heart." Smiling ironically, Jihan stood. "Well, if she really has information to sell, she'll be back. Let's put an end to the night, we begin early tomorrow."

~ 9 ~
The Heron

Aihan lit a candle from the lamp in the hall and closed the door. The shadows of the crudely made bed and straight backed chair loomed on the plank walls as he set the candle on the bedside stand. Aside from a pottery night jar and straw mat there were no other furnishings. The small window stood open to the rustling, shrilling forest and a cloud of mosquitoes.

Removing his sash he draped it over the chair back, where its embroidery reflected the candlelight as incongruously as if he had tossed a handful of silver and fire opals into Tanglevine Creek.

"Diddie, you look a mess." In a cold red dusk she stands at my door. I let her into my firelight, under the stars my man painted on the ceiling so I wouldn't pine for the rolling fields and open skies.

Her hair isn't even brushed. Her hand goes to her head. She shakes it, bewildered.

"I've seen that look, Diddie. No, not your hair, honey. Your eyes."

"In Upthegrove."

I nod.

"You'll say this isn't as bad."

I say no thing at all. I put her in a chair.

"That Officer Torran, the Domene, he been take Allie Robins' cows. Every last one. Said she owed back taxes for land she don't even own anymore." She makes a little helpless gasp, disgust, despair. "You know, that land Able and Bandor got off her last growing season—why doesn't the Domene go after those two skunks? That herd's her living! What's she gonna do?" Diddie leans forward. Her eyes spark with my firelight. "I'll give you all I got."

"What for?"

"You know what."

I say no.
"You have to help Tanglevine. You're the only
one who can."
And his guards? And the more the Fortress
will send? I turn her away.
I'm not that strong.

Unbuttoning his shirt, Jihan sat on the bed. A pungence like dried moss rose from its unyielding mattress, but tonight he could have slept soundly on the bare ground. Glancing to make sure he had bolted the door, he saw a pale corner protruding from the straw matting. Paper.

Stooping, he unfolded it. A man was drawn in thick, powdery black circles, round head on a round body, triangular skirt, scratchings for long hair and a beard. Behind him, a tree. He seemed to be flying at the height of its branches, arms outspread like a bird's wings.

Another figure gazed up at him. It had a stick body, the sex impossible to tell since there was no beard. Smiling, it seemed to hail him. The flying man was intended as a Domene in a robe, that much was clear. And he was fat. Assessor Waldis?

But what did it mean? Noticing a faint odor, Jihan raised the paper to his nose. The black marks smelled of charred wood and wild onions. Charcoal from the cooking fire.

Whoever had slid this under his door had not prepared it in advance. Some event in the public room had caused someone to—not toy with him, necessarily. Few in Tanglevine could write, judging from the marks they had made to sign Windland's list. This might be someone's best attempt to communicate anonymously.

Jihan turned the paper over, found the other side blank, and cursed. If the drawing was meant to tell him something, why could it not be clearer?

He crossed the hall to Windland's door. Knocking brought no answer. Descending the stairs he found the public room dim, a faint red from the embers showing only the two empty tables and counter. The door stood open.

The porch was also empty, but voices mixed with the night sounds. Silently he followed to the yard. The full moon dropped isolated splashes through the branches. He stayed out of the light, avoiding the trunks by touch.

One voice he knew, lazy with the rhythms of the horse country. The other, a woman's, had Tanglevine's harsh edges. "She died bitter sorry."

"She could turn me inside out like a rabbit skin." The caravan leader sounded alarmed. Or angry.

"Sun sent you."

"Or this storm of yours pulled me in. What if that's it?"

"No, we need you!"

Jihan placed the other voice. Disdaining this skulking, he strode forward. "Why do you need him?"

Dark shapes flinched away from him. Then one moved into the moonlight. The witch regarded him scornfully. "Always in the wrong place, aren't you?"

Jihan waited for her answer.

The old woman made an exasperated sound. "To help catch this killer you want, you stupid young man."

Windland's hand shot into the silver light, closing on her arm. "He won't stand much more of that, Sky. He's a Ward."

"Oh he is, is he?" Grey eyes pale as a wolf's looked him up and down, stopping at the chest hair revealed by his open shirt. She sniffed, nostrils flaring. "I don't like your feel. Name your whole name. Go on."

"Willingly," Jihan returned coldly. "It is without shame. I am Jihan son of Edwarn son of Councilor Jihan son of Council Master Edwar."

She sucked in a breath. "Your great-granddaddy was Council Master? During the War?"

"Past is past," Windland cut in. "My wife's a Domene."

Sky turned to Windland. "But your daughter's a Wisteri."

"The little'uns'll choose for themselves."

"You won't have but the one. Wife's gonna leave you."

"You don't know what you're talking about."

But she had gotten to him, and knew it. She smiled.

Windland moved between the witch and Jihan. "Like you, I took an oath. Long as Ward Jihan's in Tanglevine, me and my riders watch his back. Tell that to whoever you want."

Sky tried to shove the caravanner aside, but he did not budge. Turning her back on them both, she vanished into the darkness.

Jihan turned on his heel, leading the way across the yard. "What was her point? If she had one."

"She's worried for us."

Jihan laughed. "Worried? She hates me. Was she not trying to recruit you against me?"

Windland followed him up the steps to the dark porch. "She's not fond of you, but she says others hate you more."

"Those who killed the Assessor? What is this place, some last stronghold of outdated fanatics?"

"Arcadia's the stronghold," Windland pointed out quietly. They entered the close heat of the public room. "We in the Blue Grass don't live in the past. Just want to live and let live, most of us. But like I said, Tanglevine's a bad place."

"'Cursed?'"

"Now you've seen it, what would you say?"

"Certainly they are cursed. With poor land and lack of will. I see nothing wrong with these people that proper nourishment and education would not cure. But that would mean going where such things can be had. Why bother to take responsibility for oneself when it is so easy to blame a curse, or the Domenes?"

"Taxes fall harder than they should on Woodhollow District."

"Then I'll look into redistributing the burden." Jihan started up the staircase to the lit hallway. "Does the witch really think Waldis fell victim to old resentments? Or is that a ploy to distract you from whatever is really going on?"

Windland's straight brows slanted in a frown. "She's not lying to me. You heard, Sky's my cousin."

"The Wards of the Domed City are all related, more or less. Does that mean they should trust one another?"

Windland did not smile.

"Before you sleep, take a look at this." Jihan handed him the paper.

"A little'un's drawing?" But then he brought it closer to the lamp. "Where'd this come from?"

"Someone pushed it under my door. Probably while we were downstairs this evening."

"Waldis climbing a tree?"

"Or flying. His arms look like wings, do they not? I wonder if it's his soul flying to heaven."

"In the Blue Grass souls don't fly away. They go into the ground and water, become part of where they lived. If he's dead his soul should be at the roots of the tree."

"Waldis was not from the Blue Grass." Jihan took the paper. "This is no child's work, look how steady the lines are."

"Sky might understand it better than we do."

"Or use it to try and play up her claims. We tell her nothing. If someone wants us to know something, they will try harder, I hope. They may find you more approachable than me. I'll leave you alone briefly with each farmer we visit tomorrow. Goodnight."

Jihan shut himself in his room, slung his sword by the wall, his dagger on the far side of the pillow from the door and his clothes away, too tired to care where they fell.

But next week it's old Garnet Oaks. Tax man wants to search his house. Guards want his real silverware, maybe they want his daughter too. Garnet sent the girl to Woodhollow and shoved the Domene down his porch steps. Torran just looks at him, eyes bright in his pale, thin face.

He has his men strip Garnet in the cold and tie him to a tree. Two guards take turns flogging him. And turn. And turn about.

Maybe Garnet will live.

I give my spells all my heart, all my strength. All I've got.

My man touches my shoulder. "You've worn yourself sick. We need you strong." When I don't listen he tries reason. "Garnet's said he don't want to live. The whole world don't depend on you savin' a man that's gave up."

I look up fierce. "Oh yes it does," I say.

Sky picks among my bones.

He dreamed darkness. Moonless. Starless. Only the multitudinous whispering of the leaves. Their insupportable weight.

Borne like a lone leaf on a black stream, he caught the sweet scent of sassafras, the cucumber tang of a snake in its hole, the sharpness of pines on a ridge. Past the snuffling of a bear, past the sleepy croak of a bird he drifted, until the sky opened.

Matted branches hemmed in a tiny clearing, but its depth was fathomless, its surface the remote flicker of the stars.

At its center two sat facing inward as if toward a fire, though no fire burned. The witch again, old Sky under starry skies. She bent to something he could not see, her braid falling over her shoulder like the muscular body of a snake.

The caravan leader watched her with his arm wrapped around his knees. Sky crooned over what lay before her, a heap of herbs maybe, or feathers, and among them white stones, or maybe they were bones.

After all, there was a fire, a small one with blue tongues like flames feeding on coal vapors, but this fire fed on nothing. Not even the grass beneath burned. The witch breathed a long syllable that resonated hollowly among the ferns. The fire sent up a thin tendril.

At this, the caravanner stood. The hem of his long cloak rippled. The blue illumination touched his hair, his curved nose, his gleaming eyes. Flames licked upward, a spiral serpent ascending on itself.

Windland opened his arms as if he would clasp the column of fire. But it was no longer fire. A tall heron stood before him, white feathers glistening.

Windland let his cloak fall. Naked he stepped toward the heron and its head raised, beak curling open into water that washed shimmering over him, into flames that twined around his back and thighs, until he illuminated the grass, the branches, the crouching witch. Translucent he stood, beautiful, eerie, terrifying.

The thunder of his own heart woke him. Tense with nausea, Jihan lay in the stifling room, his heart trying to burst his ribs while the night noises mocked its rhythm and the mosquitoes whined around his sweat dampened sheet.

Wisteri Wisteri Wisteri Wisteri. That name, the witch's clan and the caravanner's, was significant. He should recall something about it, but what? Heron. That meant nothing to him. Whatever memory had brushed him, it was gone.

He woke entirely. The sickness ebbed.

It was nothing, a mere jumble of the day's impressions, each identifiable. A mosquito tickled his knuckle and he turned his hand, crushing it on the sheet.

Even if dream visions existed—which he doubted—he was not prone to them. Whatever misgivings his sleep had conjured, all was going well. Two possible informants had emerged and tomorrow's inspections might turn up something. If not, money usually worked in a poor village.

With luck he might be done by tomorrow, ready to return to Arcadia with the resolution of a touchy incident to his credit.

A rider's snore sounded through the wall.

Just as certainly, the leader was across the hall, not gallivanting in some starlit clearing but sleeping soundly, as immune to nightmares as he was to poison ivy. Jihan closed his eyes. If he did not get back to sleep himself, he would be sorry tomorrow.

~ 10 ~

Becks Hollow

awn pokes out a feeler. Sun finds me! He touches me with rays, they warm me, skitter like little skeeters over my skin. I brush a tender tickle of grass on my cheek, then run run run, feet soles bruising on rocks, shaley ones that flake in gritties sharp between my toes.

I stick my nose in the crotch of an oak. Never noticed before how it smells of roasted chicory— with ants!

I find a woodpecker's feather and blow it tumble jumble against the breeze, I hear a bumblebee, I spy her yellow and black stripes among the jewelweed and with my fingertip I pet her fuzzles. There you bee! You see me?

I leap over the man that's asleep on the grass and I bend down to the old witch and give her a smacking kiss. I crow, "Look what you've let loose now!"

Fear comes into her eyes.

I smile. She wants a promise, but I know what promises are worth.

Fair warning, little'uns mine. Whatever comes next, on your heads be it. Too late to stop me now. And way, way too late to stop the storm.

Sky opens, wind blows, let's see which way the tangled vine grows.

The toil to get from one farm to the next, the sheer solitude of such a life, oppressed increasingly as the day wore on and the clouds mounted, and the hot burden of the humidity bore down.

At each stop a farmer recounted only an ordinary inspection by Assessor Waldis, and though they saw his tracks, even found a broken pen he had discarded, they learned nothing useful. One farmer quoted what she claimed was his estimate. That he would give one verbally was as unlikely as the figure she named.

But Jihan had expected such chicanery. What he did not expect was the ferocity of the damages, entire crops washed out, breakwaters ripped open and livestock carried away, a barn lurching with its posts protruding like broken ribs.

Most disturbing of all was the impression of irrational, but deliberate, intention, a fallow field bypassed while the farmed one next to it was devastated, flood water defying gravity to fling itself up a hillside and drench a house, uprooted trees strewn over a valley like twigs.

"Must of seemed like the end of the world," Arn remarked.

"And sounded like the opening of Hell." The last several hours had doubled Jihan's dislike of this chaotic wilderness of snaring vines, man-high ferns and teeming insects. He nodded at the crop of corn lying prone in the damp slime. "Well, we can rule out one theory. No feuding gangs did this."

"Oh, there's the pretty smell." Camellia pointed across the field. The flood had knocked a fence askew and a dead bull hung over it. The stench was indeed noticeable. Jihan considered it a measure of this place's repulsiveness that he had not separated the odor from his other impressions.

"Yet Diddie couldn't give us a decent meal," said Arn.

Camellia wrinkled her nose. "You'd rather she served us that?"

"She's saving it for your dessert," Arn rejoined, but turned to Windland. "You don't see, do you? But you three never grew up in a poor village. In mine, that much beef'd keep a family for a long time. Why would they let it rot?"

Windland considered. "Dogs didn't touch it either," he said at last. "Or buzzards."

Jihan shifted impatiently. His bay started and he had to turn it in a quick circle. "Don't say it," he warned.

Windland shrugged.

Jihan frowned. "We have seen nothing that cannot be explained by perfectly natural causes. The bull may have been too diseased to eat, or too difficult to reach until the flood receded. As for the capriciousness of the storm, have you considered a tornado? I have read that a tornado's funnel may touch the earth only intermittently. Its damage can look willful, but it is not. Tornados have been known to siphon water from streams and drop it miles away."

"Whatever kind of storm it was, rain's coming." Windland pointed at the darkening clouds. "Let's get done at Marcy Beck's before it starts."

Jihan's teeth met in annoyance. He had forgotten that side trip. A waste of time. Unless the villagers were lying, Assessor Waldis had not even visited that farm.

However, he had given his word, so map in hand he led the way along Tanglevine Creek to its headwaters in Becks Hollow, where the villagers' markings showed half a dozen farms belonging to the Becks clan. People working in a field directed them to a side path above the hollow proper, leading toward its narrow upper end.

Their hooves sound nearer, heavy on the sodden ground. Like a nightmare where there's no waking. No way out, no escape, no end to the circle of blindness, and hatred, the fate I've shaped. Or that has shaped me.

Which is it? Does it matter?

No escape.

The sky before them loomed darker than the wooded hills. Vines looped across the water, clogged with debris from former floods. A fallen tree lay sodden as a sponge, grown with vivid orange fungi and whitish nodules on hair-thin feelers. No birds called. All was silent but the secretive gurgling of the water.

The trail bent, revealing a bowl of a clearing so small it was more an enclosure than an opening. A cabin perched on the near hillside, its front on stilts.

"Let's not bother Marcy," Windland told his riders. "There's the shed." Beyond a pen where three chickens pecked it stood, the felled tree slanting across its roof. Someone had made a half-hearted start on chopping it up. Exposed wood gleamed bright beneath the darkening clouds.

With a wordless cry Camellia kicked her horse to a gallop around the pen, halted sharply and dropped from the saddle into the high grass. Following, Jihan saw a crushed patch, and the red of churned ground. Then he saw the boy.

His chest was ripped open. Flies buzzed noisily there. The child's arms seemed too long, as if they had been stretched. His face was unmarked against the mud, the only blood where the small white teeth had bitten. Milk teeth, Jihan remembered women called them, but in his agony they had bitten clear through his lip.

Jihan had thought war had hardened him to sights of death, but he could not look at this. He turned away.

And saw the mother. She lay in running position, arms reaching for the boy, but her foremost leg was bent the wrong way, snapped at the knee. Her mouth gaped. If not for the frizzy brown hair he would not have recognized her. Marcy's forehead and eyes were caved to a congealed mass where flies feasted.

Camellia looked up silently as he and Windland dismounted.

Arn rounded on Windland. "What the hell did this to them?"

Windland knelt between the dead girl and child. His back tense, he bit his finger and traced a circle over each. Rising he clasped Camellia's shoulder, then faced the vine-strewn thickets of the nearest slope thoughtfully.

"They'll be long gone by now," Arn told him. "This happened hours ago."

"At least," Windland agreed. He turned, slowly looking over the ground in all directions. A pensive "huh" escaped him.

Jihan's eyes were drawn irresistibly back to the savagery. He felt his fist close around the pommel of his sword. Anger hardened cold in his vitals. His gorge rose with the force of it, a pressure that grew until silence was no longer possible. He controlled his voice, but the fury thickened it. "This cannot be borne."

~ II ~

Partners

The vine-knotted undergrowth did not stir. Clouds mounted. In the distance a bird called. Windland considered the crushed grass and mud on all sides of the dead woman and child. At last he asked, "What do you make of it?"

"Nobody but a crazy person could do this," Camellia declared with force. "Or possessed."

"Frenzy," Jihan agreed, "but perhaps not obvious madness. I've seen battle drive soldiers into rampages. I once gave way to a red rage myself when an ally turned traitor. But this is the Domelands, not some savage battlefield." He looked down at what was left of the girl's face. "These killers must not escape justice."

"Killers? More than one, you think?" Windland asked.

Bending, Jihan lifted the child's arms. "He was gripped, see the bruises. That one held no weapon, he merely grasped and wrenched. The ribs broke and sliced the chest. A large man, I'd say, and strong." The flaccidness of the dislocated arms was sickening. He laid them gently by the boy's sides. "But the woman was bludgeoned. Someone stood between her and the child, preventing her reaching him."

"She's reaching for him still." Camellia turned, not letting them see her tears.

"Could be just one," argued Arn, "He kills the woman, drops the weapon, grabs the boy."

"Either way, something's missing," Windland said.

"The bludgeon," answered Jihan.

"That too. It's footprints I'm thinking of. Or hoof marks. There's the little'un's tracks coming from the house." Windland pointed. "Here comes Marcy around the pen. See how deep her heels dig—she's running—but do you see any others?"

Jihan examined the ground again. The mud was soft, the damp grass not resilient. Their own prints were as clear as those of the dead. "I see none, but I'm not a skilled tracker."

"You?" Windland asked the riders. They shook their heads.

"They didn't fly," Jihan returned in irritation, but the drawing came to his mind, Waldis flapping among the branches. "Nor did the Assessor," he muttered.

Windland turned sharply to him. "See a connection?"

"No," Jihan admitted. He opened his mind to random thoughts, hunches. None came. "Quarter the farm," he told the two riders. "Look for tracks, the weapon, blood, anything at all that seems unusual. Windland and I will search the house."

Their screaming echoes against the hills. The earth, the water, the very air remembers. I left Upthegrove to escape the echoes echoes echoes of the screaming, but the whole world is a jagged blade. Marcy comes running, and again she's too late. Again and again, mocking the forever circling of the Sun.

What have I done?

If I taste the bark of a tree, the honey of a bee, beneath is the reek of blood.

Breeze in the grass. A woodpecker's knocking. Buzzing of flies.

Then—don't you just know? Here they come like little wooden wheelie toys on a string, bay horse and chestnut side by side. Domene and Blue Grass, partners—like brothers, you'd think. They spot Marcy and her little'un.

Poor ol' Marcy who once stole my hair ribbon then was gom-brained enough to wear it to Diddie's stay. Made her sorry for it, didn't I?

Off their horses, staring, gawking, gesturing. Storm threatens black over the trees. Draw the circle, Cousin Windland, see how you're both being used.

Ha, he does! Now, don't you dare tell the Domene! And he doesn't. That's my sweet cousin, incandescent in the night.

But some people, anger makes their eyes burn dark. That's the Domene. Sucks his cheeks too, don't he look scary! Such a fine brash thoroughbred he is, so fierce, so splendid.

If his passion was the other kind, think what a treat he'd be. Breathing hard like that, with his uptilty eyes a glitter and his eyebrows arched so sharp you could break yourself on 'em. And that long hair flowing over his strong shoulders!

Now he grips that sword of his. Bet it's killed its share and more.

What if he had Marcy's murderers now? Would they live to stand trial?

Only, my guess is he'd haul 'em to the Fortress. All Domenes strut, some go maverick, but they don't get power by running wild. This one's got power, anybody can see that in the pride of his stance, in the lift of his head.

He's so sure of himself, this one. It makes him such apt bait. So completely predictable.

Except.

Except I didn't expect this. The way he looks down at them lying there. How completely he means it when he vows justice. Not because this slaughter crosses his authority. He must feel it all spinning out of his control, it must nittle him, but it's Marcy and Poke that get to him. After all he's seen, after all he's done, after all he probably will do.

Could've said, well what'd they expect, addle-noggin girl and her bastard living up the holler all alone. But he doesn't. He says, This cannot be borne.

What's in this Domene that wasn't in the others?

Not that I trust him. Not a bit. Not a speck. Not a spot on a tick!

But a little Outlander girl and her brat, lowest of the low.

Yet he cares.

And the way his lips parted, the way he panted when he woke in his sweated sheets.

When he dreamed of me.

Oh, it comes over me so swift, all I should've seen coming! Yet it takes me by surprise. What I have to do. All I'll have to risk. The price I may have to pay. My finding cry splits the clouds. I take wing and fly away over the hill.

The clouds rolled away into the mountains, removing their threat of rain. The villagers walked up to Becks Hollow. Only Diddie's younger son remained to serve the roasted pork bought with the money Jihan had advanced.

The insects droned on. Two of the riders' voices wafted from the stable. Tal and Daw were still out searching the road for signs of Waldis.

"What if their deaths were aimed at somebody else?" Windland leaned back in a porch chair, beer beside him. His eyes reflected the leafy light.

"The child's father, for instance," Jihan speculated. "I wonder who he is. Finding out may not be easy."

"Could be a deep dark secret," Windland agreed. "—If Tanglevine was Domene." He leaned toward the open door. "Know who sired Marcy's little'un?" he called.

"Bandor Coves," came Diddie's son's matter of fact answer.

"There's a lot to be said for taking love as it comes." Windland settled back in his chair. "A Coves," he mused.

"Most interesting," Jihan agreed. "A clan likely enough to make enemies, I'd think. But who are Bandor Coves' enemies? Does Blue Grass forthrightness extend that far?"

The adolescent appeared, polishing a mug. "Nobody likes Bandor. Long time he been cheat people of their land."

"Little pitchers have big ears." Windland gave the boy an amused smile. "What else can you tell us about Bandor Coves?"

"That he's ogly as sin." Plainly, the boy was enjoying their attention.

"Whose land did he take?" Jihan asked.

"Rass Oaks'. Some belongin' to the Robins, I think, dunno who all's. Him and ol' Able Lasts, nobody'd shed tears if they wandered up Lost Creek."

Jihan frowned. "Lost Creek?"

"You know, died."

"I see." Jihan sipped his beer in thought. The boy got bored and went inside.

Windland propped his feet on the porch rail. "What about Assessor Waldis?"

"What of him?"

"Some'd say he's the one who's your business here.

"Waldis will get his turn, but his trail is cold. The girl and child are no less Arcardia's responsibility. If their lives are worth nothing, what is the Domed City's honor worth? What is my own honor worth?"

"You're a hothead, Ward Jihan. I thought cold, but she had you right."

"Who?"

"The witch." Windland sipped his beer and made a face at its insubstantiality. A beam of the sunset escaped the clouds, casting leafy shadows on the porch. He set his mug down. "That why they took away your command?"

"What?" But then Jihan recalled his own subterfuge. He preferred not to lie to this man, but he did not yet feel certain of him. He sifted for plausible bits of the truth. "Conflict with City Council has shaped my career," he admitted. "My father was Master of the Outlands until he ran afoul of a Council struggle."

Windland nodded. Then his eyes widened. "*He* was your father? Edwarn Road Builder?"

"So they called him, until he was forced to resign."

The caravan leader seemed to find this interesting. "I remember. Misappropriating funds, wasn't it? But I heard the charges were trumped up."

"Exactly," Jihan confirmed. "Nothing was ever proved."

Tradition upheld certain privileges, and his father had abused them no more than his accusers had. "But his position had already been undermined. It was really the sabotage of the Great Road that ended his career."

"Don't remember a lot about that." The insects' rasps nearly drowned Windland's quiet voice. "Pretty much before my time."

Jihan shot him a covert glance. The Office of Trade required seven years' apprenticeship before a rider could apply for a leader's license. According to Arcadia's files, Windland had led caravan for four years, making eleven at least— the year of the sabotage. As an apprentice he may have had no hand in it, but if the saboteurs were caravanners as suspected, he probably knew more than he pretended.

"Who laid the charges scarcely matters now," Jihan answered. Another half truth. "It's clear which Councilors encouraged and protected them."

"Is Edwarn Road Builder still alive?"

Jihan smiled bitterly. He might as well be dead for all the Outlands cared now. "He lives in retirement in the house once called his, but which most now call mine. He has his books, his grandsons, he plays chess with my wife and the few friends who have not deserted him."

"The Council threw away a man—a Ward at that—for one failed dream?"

Jihan nodded. "Such waste is not uncommon in Council. Twenty-five Wards hold shares in the City, but there are only eleven Council seats. Under those conditions, opponents' hostilities can be implacable." His father's dream had antagonized too many, had been pursued too openly. *Learn from my mistake, Han,* his father had warned, bidding him farewell for the Blue Grass. *Do not reveal your intentions until they are facts.*

"So you had to rise the hard way. The war."

"The only way. The family name is tarnished. I mean to restore it."

"Already have, haven't you? Your victories at Eagle Rocks and Tauton? They say your troops'd do anything for you, and not just because you usually won. Because you led from the front."

Jihan sipped his beer. "Would you ask your riders to do what you wouldn't do?"

Windland smiled. An acknowledgement.

"I wonder when the villagers will return."

"They'll bury their dead now, at sunset. We'll get no chance to question the family tonight, they'll wake by the grave. Bandor too, maybe. The rest'll probably gather here."

"We may not need Bandor. His partner, this Able Lasts, can probably tell us about his enemies."

"Like, which ones go without footprints?"

Jihan frowned. "That will have an explanation."

"And if it doesn't? Shouldn't we at least think about that?"

"What, and consult the witch?"

"Might not hurt."

"Hunt monsters if you can't help yourself," Jihan answered. "I'm after living men."

~ 12 ~

The Dancer

orches cast orange streaks among the trees. Voices sounded as the lights were dowsed in the creek and the public room began to fill. Diddie lit few lamps, leaving all in a softened gloom.

The table near the counter was occupied by the notables of Tanglevine, some of the farmers now familiar, the blacksmith, the shopkeeper and others. Diddie, who moved among them with beer and food, also seemed high in village regard. Others settled for the less comfortable table by the hearth, the young, and the more ragged. Jihan spotted the two "flibbertygibbets" who had mocked them on their arrival, this time snickering at the farmers. He did not see the witch.

He and Windland listened as unobtrusively as possible from the end of the first table. The riders did the same by the hearth, except for Arn who was tending to the horses. When Diddie came by with fried apples, Jihan asked, "Is Bandor Coves here?"

"Nobody been know where Bandor's got to." Her stance accused the man.

"What of Able Lasts?"

"Over there." She jerked her head at the hearth. "Tall'un with the twitchy hands. Why?"

Jihan saw him, topping most by a head, but unlike the Coves he was gaunt. His hand curled around his beer mug, and as she said, his fingers twitched. His skin was yellowish. As Jihan watched, his mouth abruptly jerked down in a grimace that did not affect the rest of his face. "He is Bandor's friend, is he not?"

She considered. "Been close since they's little'uns, but it's beyond me to say. Some bad blood's between 'em. I don't ask what. Those two ain't but trouble."

"But they are partners?"

She nodded.

Windland looked up at her. "You blame Bandor."

"Me and others. Bandor Coves took advantage of Marcy because she was how she was. Treated her like the dirt on his shoe bottoms. He's got a wife—Song Becks over there."

Jihan caught Windland's startled glance.

"Marcy was alone, needin' his help, but precious nothing did she get 'cept from her own kin, poor as they are. Bandor, he's got land. Song been help Marcy and Poke a little, but those Coves, they're mean as water moccasins and Bandor's the lowest of all the Coves."

"Now he's remorsed, though," remarked a woman nearby who had been listening. "Did you see it? Bandor of all people, weeping tears. Couldn't even bear to stay, just stumbled off while we been sing. Ais' me, Bandor Coves is a broken man."

Diddie nodded. "Finally knows he did wrong."

"Remorse all he wants, too late now."

Another possibility occurred to Jihan. An ugly one.

Chaos, back to chaos times. Misshapen shadows instead of living.

When brute greed's got the law on its side, and brute force is the law, and there's nothing but death in the smell of the wind, and nothing in the heart but what's dead or dying.

Garnet Oaks only tried to protect what he loved.

And Berry Rivers in Shadetree sued a Domene for stealing her horse, so the Fortress took all her foals for slaughter.

And Fared, sweet Fared's head upended by the wall. A Domene kicked it out of his way.

And what about my Deer? What about my baby girl, is she a toy for the Provincial Guard in some drunk or murderous moment?

When saving what's left becomes everything.

There is a way to power, witches whisper among themselves. A way, but it's forbidden. Obscene. Damned, damning for eternity.

I would take that on myself if I could save my home, my people, my child. No one's tried it since the chaos times. But no one's had enough magic to try mastering so much power. I've passed my teachers. I'm the strongest witch in the Blue Grass, but here I sit like a groundhog in a hole. If I do nothing for them, I'm worse than damned.

Let chaos come! Fill me with hate because hate's the only love. There is no protection but destruction, so let a rage of destruction mount in me! Let it pour from my mouth when I shout, from my eyes when I look, from my thoughts when I think on driving these murderers and robbers from my land.

I will rise like a storm cloud and I will fill myself with power and I will throw fear and darkness and a plague on the Domenes and all who aid them.

Arn made his way to their table. "Ward, your horse is favoring his off foreleg. It's cool, no filling, couldn't find anything lodged in his hoof, but maybe it's a stone bruise."

The last thing he needed. "How lame is it?"

"If you have to ride him tomorrow, better go easy. Windland here's a wonder with touch." He glanced at the leader. "Got time?"

Silently cursing the delicacy of thoroughbreds, Jihan nodded permission to Windland, who rose and went out. Arn followed him. Their only extra horses were two pack nags, and the village was unlikely to have any better. Jihan considered whose mount to commandeer if his own proved unsound. Not the red mare. Windland's good will was important, perhaps for long after this expedition. Arn's raw gelding had power.

Another entered, a man broad across the chest with dark hair and thick brows. People looked up, but the newcomer crossed straight to the counter. In the resuming talk Jihan heard the name Bandor.

Beer in hand, Bandor Coves joined his wife Song Becks and others of Covesian cast of feature. He did not speak to them, nor they to him, though Song watched with concern.

Her name did not suit her. She was more aged than her husband and Jihan thought he detected the anxious attention to his every move typical of women accustomed to beatings. Bandor fit the picture of a crude, probably brutal, man.

But what could provoke such insane viciousness as had been let loose on Marcy and her child? Jealousy was perhaps an answer, but these people were not given to sexual possessive-ness—or so it was claimed.

For now, Jihan held off from approaching him, giving beer and the company of his kin a chance to turn the man's mood. After a while, Able Lasts made his way to the Coves.

Bandor broke his silence. His voice was only an indistinct growl among the others, but Able squeezed his shoulder in answer. Mouth contorting to a one-sided grin that contradicted the earnestness in the rest of his face, Able leaned to Bandor, talking urgently. Both glanced at Jihan. Their recoil when they saw him watching intrigued him. It was time to move in on them.

Diddie blocked his way, pitcher in hand. "The dancer's come." She paused as if that meant something.

At Jihan's inquiring look she explained, "We have an old way here. When one of us dies, our village witch remembers the dead and dances 'em home if they're lost. It's not a thing we let strangers see, but we been hear you vowed justice for Marcy and Poke. Our witch, she says you can stay."

Checking his annoyance, Jihan scraped up the necessary courtesy. "I am honored." He settled back on the bench. At least Sky was unlikely to have much stamina. The delay would be brief, and Bandor and Able did not look like going anywhere.

A man sitting on the stairs fit together two sections of a wooden flute. As he raised it, people quieted. A fall of notes trembled through the room, surprisingly melodic, lacking the resonance of a Domene flute but thin and sweet

as if heard in the distance. It was a strange key
the wandering notes established, neither minor
nor major, haunting as breezes wavering through
the woods. Jihan was a passable musician, quick
at picking up tunes on his travels, but this was
unlike any he knew.

A motion at the porch door drew his eye.
White swirled as the dancer entered, not Sky but
a younger woman with hair like burnished
copper.

She moved with slow, sinuous grace, her
steps decorous, but hinting at sensuousness.
Who could imagine Tanglevine contained a
woman of such bearing? Head in profile, she
arched her neck, one shoulder circling then the
other, the movements continuing down her
slender torso and back as if she were as insub-
stantial as a shaft of light through a running
stream.

She turned as the flute quickened to a
rhythm of five beats, arms lifting, soft white
scarves flaring from her wrists and elbows, white
veiling drifting about her body, falling from one
shoulder to flow over the small roundness of her
breasts, then parting as she lifted and straightened a long, neatly muscled leg. Balancing easily,
she stretched her arms before her, bending over
the horizontal leg like some pale butterfly
folding on a flower.

It was indeed a dance suited to the memory of a young and simple woman, delicate as a dream as yet unshaped, wistful as hopes scarcely sensed. Even he, who had not known the girl, was moved from pity and anger to a profound regret for the life that now would never unfurl.

The dancer wove between the tables and stairs as the flute shifted to a major key. Her delight in her motion grew, it glowed in her blue-grey eyes, it startled itself with a brief O of her mouth, as pleased as a child inventing some new play. Her spinning was all knees and elbows now, her daring a boy's, facing danger with a sword of air and this time vanquishing it, rounding off the victory with a throaty shout.

Then, eyes closing, smiling, she melted into a shivering downward scale, into silence, into stillness.

No one moved. Gradually Jihan grew aware of a low hum. It dwelt on no one note, nor had any prearranged tune. Each person found a pitch that changed only slowly, bass and treble voices blending in a strangely harmonic dissonance like the reverberations of harp strings without stops.

The dancer lifted her head, her hands. Her supple breasts were outlined against the soft white. Her hair flowed down her back as she quivered to the hum. Her navel was a shadow in her firm belly. She was a feather borne on air, a new leaf.

Though she scarcely moved, she thrilled as vibrantly as if currents of breath, streams of water, flowing life, passed through her body. Jihan's cock stirred as the veiling clung to her uptilted nipples and she turned her rapt face upward. Her lips parted slightly as if to some lover's touch, her entire being an ecstatic welcome.

Whether it was a homecoming for the dead, or a hope for some new rebirth, or reconciliation to some wholeness beyond death and loss, Jihan did not know. He only knew a fleeting but passionate wish that her welcome was for him.

But no such thing. What he watched was no tavern entertainment. He knew that he was seeing a ritual, some remnant of the old, forbidden beliefs that had once united the people of this province and held them stubbornly together against all the strength of the Domed City.

This was the flavor of that strange mingling of religious and sensual desire that rendered them unable to distinguish between their land, their gods and their passions. To those who believed that the land and people, death and life, fertility and relinquishing made an unending circle, what loss was to be feared? They had resisted the breaking of that circle for nearly forty years, to uncounted costs in Domene lives and funds. Bent to the wrong ends, love was a dangerous force.

All too seductive, such beliefs. And all too close to a hypnotic spell, this art that remembered those old, wild passions. No wonder Domene law had banned such rituals. Now they were long-extinct, or so it was thought.

Jihan realized how excited certain Masters of Learning would be to discover that was not quite so, that in this obscure place, the final echoes had not quite died out. They would give much for the glimpse of history he had just seen.

But he also knew he would not report it for their dissecting pens. In this strange, remote place, let the last remnant of a dead beauty fade in peace.

The dancer lowered her arms. Her eyes opened as the villagers' hum silenced. Her gaze rested on his face. Jihan's breath caught, but she turned and left the inn, her weariness revealed in the willowy droop of her shoulders and head.

The gathering sat in silence. Perhaps they were remembering the dead. Perhaps they felt the enchantment of the dance. And the dancer, he admitted to himself.

Aside from her skill, she was not really so extraordinary, only attractive in a common enough Blue Grass way, fine boned with red tints in the hair and rose in the skin, blue or grey eyed, with a hint of the elf or elemental. Windland, Sky, the Becks and Lissas families in Tanglevine, were all of that type.

Yet this one…

Best not to dwell on it.

But he had reasons besides lust to wonder about her. When the innkeeper passed, he complimented the dance. "I did not see your dancer at the meeting last night."

"I don't recall she was there."

"She's your village witch, you say?"

"Powerful'un."

"What of Sky? She said she was Tanglevine's witch."

Diddie thought it over, frowning. "She is."

"Rivals?"

Diddie considered that. Then her frown unknotted. "No now, grandmother and grand-daughter. If it's a witch you're wanting, here's Sky." She pointed at the door where the old woman stood peering in at the gathering.

"No, thank you."

Bandor rose. Able's hand shook as he grasped the heavier man's arm. He spoke urgently, his voice rising but his words indistinct among the others' voices.

Bandor's answer did not carry, but he tried to shake off the man's grip. Able bunched his shirt in a yellow fist. "Betrayal, that's what! He's got no right to the heron."

Bandor muttered something and knocked his partner's fist away so hard he gave a pained grunt. Rubbing his hand, Able stepped over the bench and stalked out, mouth jerking.

Swiftly Jihan rose and crossed the room in a few strides, intercepting Bandor. "Spare me a moment."

Bandor Coves met his look steadily. His eyes were as opaque as two black pebbles. His black brows lowered. "No."

"What if we want the same thing? Tell me about—"

"Say Marcy Becks and I'll kill you where you stand." Bandor pushed past him to the porch.

"Nevertheless, tomorrow we will speak of Marcy Becks."

Bandor wheeled, hand closing on his knife.

Jihan did not move. The man only hoped to intimidate him. If he had meant to use it the motion would not have been so obvious.

They exchanged stare for stare. "In the morning I will inspect your wife's farm," Jihan said. "Be there."

Bandor cursed him and went heavily down the steps. Jihan remained on the porch. "How does Windland betray his heron tattoo?"

Bandor turned. "By bein' a fuckbrained fool. If you trust him you're another'n." He stumped down the path.

"Able Lasts is fond of you." Jihan leaned causally on the stall door.

Windland looked up from where he knelt in the straw. "What's he want, meet me in some shady grove?"

"There's an attractive thought."

Windland smiled, but tiredness shadowed his eyes. When the bay moved restlessly he made a soothing sound, the flats of his fingers moving slowly upward along the horse's foreleg.

"He and Bandor argued. I think you had better watch your back."

"All I need." The caravanner sighed.

"The word 'betrayal' was spoken. Able seems to think your tattoo sorts ill with your position as my assistant."

"Blue Grass, Domene, why can't they leave off? I'm sick of it." His fingers released and moved down. The young stallion held still, his ears relaxed. "I get it in the Caverns too. So does Simura."

Jihan said nothing. Domene prejudice might be expressed less forthrightly, but he could not claim it was less strong.

"You too, ain't?" Windland asked the horse. "You're Domene, but Blue Grass-born, 'eah?" Its eyelids drooped with pleasure. The caravanner looked up at Jihan, his eyes half-closed too, but with weariness. "Only, horses can't choose. I chose to ride caravan for the Domed City, Simura chose me. Now we've got to live with it."

"Yet, the choice has proven difficult for one with the heron on his body?"

Windland smiled. "You been thinking about my body?"

The attempt to nettle him from his purpose was obvious. Plainly, he was not going to get an answer. The tattoo was some closely guarded local secret, perhaps yet another trace of some old superstition.

Maybe the Wisteri were a witch clan. Windland's skill at healing by touch was evident in the bay's slack lip and flopped ears. Well, let him keep his family secret, so long as he remained loyal to his duty. Jihan settled for a retort in kind. "Do not imagine you're Tanglevine's heart throb. Tonight you missed a far finer sight. The old witch has a grand-daughter, it turns out. She did a dance for the dead."

Windland glanced up. "'Eah?"

"With skill and grace. Much grace."

"Too bad I missed it, then."

"Yes, I think you would have appreciated it," Jihan mused. "But maybe she'll dance again before we leave—for some happier occasion, let us hope."

"Maybe so." Windland looked up at him with more attention. His fingers circled where pastern joined hoof. "But then, dancers and such can be trouble. Come to think, maybe I'll steer clear of her."

"Oh?" Jihan smiled. "Are you so certain you are not Domene, after all?"

"My wife's got Domene notions about marriage." Windland stood, giving the bay a soft slap on the shoulder. "I try not to hurt her."

"Our way is difficult at times," Jihan acknowledged. He knew there was no worthy reason for his gratification at Windland's lack of interest in the dancer. But he felt it, all the same. "My thanks for your attentions to my horse."

They returned to the inn together in silence.

~ 13 ~

Possession

Blood. They lay bleeding, the child and Marcy Becks, scarcely more than a child, herself. Flies swarmed and the stench rose. "What I want to know," said Arn, leaning on the wreckage of a fence, "why didn't they cut 'em up and serve 'em while they were fresh?"

Windland gave a noncommittal shrug. Head tilted to one side, he regarded the murdered girl and child with disinterest. But surely it was Windland who should be driven by pity, wrath, the need to protect his countrymen? Was it not the Blue Grass provincial who should vow justice, hurl some old local curse, pursue the villagers until he had the murderers by the throats?

But Windland's mouth indented in the hint of a smile. "It's just war, Commander Jihan. Your job's finding Assessor Waldis."

Waldis was lost. In a cavern chamber he lay, at the star studded roots of the world. His robe was drenched and muddy and his wrists were bound, his thin arms stretched wide. Blood matted his black hair, but he was not dead. Not yet.

His eyes stared, pupils expanding to fill the dark irises as his heart labored, bulging and contracting horribly, beating exposed in his open chest. His mouth gaped in a long, high scream. "Waldis," Jihan shouted, struggling against the clawing branches to reach him.

He jerked awake.

A second scream echoed from the hillsides. Windland's door banged open, and the riders'. Footsteps pounded in the hallway. Jihan pulled his trousers hurriedly over his nightshirt, grabbed his sword and ran down the stairs.

Nothing moved in the yard but the disquieted moonlight. Then a lantern pierced the trees, and another. Voices echoed along the stream.

Jihan followed, at first seeing only yellow reflections blazing in the water, but then he made out villagers collecting in a rough crescent, its open side toward the creek.

There a lone figure faced them, a woman with her arms raised clumsily. She was sodden to the thighs of her pants, and mud clotted her hair. "Marcy!" someone murmured in superstitious awe, but it was not Marcy. It was the flibberty-gibbet with the short, ungainly body and pimpled skin, the one with a liking for green eyes.

Yet, it was not her face. Jihan thought of the face from his nightmare, but it was not agony that distorted the girl's blank eyes and thin lipped, gaping mouth. It was virulent hatred.

"Come get me." Her tongue slurped on the words, but they were discernible. In one raised fist metal gleamed. A knife.

Some of the villagers edged closer, but she snarled. Blade jabbing the air, she cursed them in a monotone like stones hurled one after another, a hailstorm of mindless fury.

Two farmers' eyes met. One moved toward her and when she lunged the other caught her, but did not succeed in pinning the knife arm. With a shriek she tried to plunge the blade into him, and when she could not, into herself.

The first farmer caught it and wrenched it away. It clattered on the creek's rocky edge, a wicked thing, rusty, with no haft but a dirty rag wrapped around the tang. The girl went spinning in the other direction toward the riders, saw Windland and sprang at him. Three others caught her. One was Sky. "Put this in her mouth," the witch ordered. "Don't let her swallow her tongue." They bore the girl to the ground and the witch forced a brown powder past the wood they had stuck between her teeth like a bit.

"Get back," Sky warned a grey haired man and woman who hovered near. "You can't take her home yet—give me room."

All withdrew a little but for the two holding her down. Jihan found the other flibbertygibbet standing by him, gulping with tears. He stepped forward, but Sky waved him back and beckoned Windland instead. The caravanner knelt at the girl's head as he had knelt earlier to tend the horse.

The witch laid arthritic fingers on the girl's forehead. "What do you want?"

A gurgle came from the open mouth. Her teeth clenched on the wood, her neck tendons standing rigid as if with lockjaw.

"Who you want to hurt?"

The eyes rolled back. Her mouth fell open and the wood slid out.

"Herbs are working now, you can let go," the witch told the farmers. Dubiously one released her, and when she did nothing the other also moved back. Windland placed his fingers on her throat, feeling her pulse. "Still racing?" Sky asked. He nodded.

"Look around," the old woman commanded. "Who do you want to talk to?"

"Got nothin' to say," the girl mumbled, eyes focusing with difficulty not on any of the gathering but the shadowy leaves above. "Gonna hear him beg me first."

"Who?"

"Gonna rub his blood on the rocks." She laughed tonelessly. "All the rocks between here and Torran's Well."

"How d'you aim to catch him?"

"This is pointless," Jihan growled, causing some of the villagers to start. He turned to the man and woman he took for her parents. "The day's shock, that is what ails her. She needs rest, not sorcery and hounding."

They feared for her, he could see that, but they only stared helplessly, doing nothing. "Hush up," Sky snapped. She fed the girl more powder, making her cough and drool brown foam.

Windland stroked her forehead. "What happened to Waldis?" he asked quietly.

A gob of brown spit hit him on the chin. "Bled him like a pig! Crows got his eyes!"

"Where is he?"

"Lost Creek—where you'll all go!"

Windland and Sky exchanged a look. Jihan moved closer.

The girl laughed, a hollow sound. The water over the rocks seemed to echo it. "I ain't finished," she taunted Sky. "I'm just starting. Ain't nothing you can do about me, and you know it. You know who called me up."

"Cease this," Jihan told them, disgusted.

Her eyes flicked to him. "I'm gonna slit his belly, make him eat his own guts and you're gonna watch." She giggled.

"Do you intend to continue this madness all night?"

"Yes," Sky answered, "if it doesn't let her go."

"There is no 'it'."

A triumphant yell burst from the girl. She went limp. Her eyes closed. Sky looked at Windland. "It's gone." From her pocket she took the green lump of a rolled leaf. She opened it, pinched some of the dried petals it held, and put them between the girl's lips while Windland soothed her forehead. Jihan stalked back to the inn.

Windland had not shut his door when he hurried out. Diddie seemed honest enough, but the inn stood open to all. For a semblance of security at least, Jihan closed the door. As he did,

he saw two packs by the narrow bed. On one lay
Arn's floppy hat.

That was a shock.

Unexpected, anyway.

Though why, Jihan did not know. Signs had
been there. Windland's lack of interest in the
dancer, for one thing. Arn's constant, unspoken
support might be the loyalty of a rider for his
leader, but he was always there, Windland's
shadow, a waif not effeminate but despite his
toughness not manly either. Communication
between the two was such an implicit shorthand
that they rarely needed to speak in full
sentences, and mere glances served as often as
words.

Jihan had taken it for the ease of two who
had worked together for years, and so it no
doubt was. Among other things.

Why should it shock him? What did it
matter?

It did not, of course. The Outlander's
unsavory predilections were his own business,
and his fall to temptation—or his hypocrisy—
had no bearing on the work in Tanglevine.

Except that Jihan had thought he was
coming to know the caravan leader, to sense
what to expect from him.

To trust him.

It was a warning. Full trust would be unwise. Not because of the man's tastes, because of his deceptions.

Jihan shut himself in his room, letting the bar fall with a bang. Feigning to honor his wife's feelings, Windland had a bedfellow. Pretending he only half believed in local superstitions, he was working with the witch. Had not his own dreams warned him of as much?

Putting down the candle he had lit in the hall, Jihan propped his sword by the bed. Weak, all of them. Lacking in principles. Not born inferior, maybe, but seriously wanting in backbone, and that was formed only by proper training from youth on. Though he liked Windland, he was still learning about these people. He would heed this lesson.

Jihan lay on the hard mattress, sleepless now. He craved the relaxing massage he was used to receiving before bedtime from his manservant, who by now must have reached Arcadia. Lacking that comfort, he would have gladly settled for a simple, straightforward conversation with anyone at all, provided they were sane and Domene.

Instead, he saw the berzerking girl's outstretched arms behind his closed eyelids, like Waldis' skinny arms in his dream, bound and stretched. Stretched grotesquely, like the boy Poke's.

Jihan frowned. He turned over. Then he rose. Retrieving his pack, he hunted through it until finding the folded paper, he opened it to the candle light. The tree. Waldis with his arms outstretched among the branches. Not flying. Bound.

In a tree? By no stretch of the imagination was this a drawing of the cave from his nightmare. Water flowed from the cave, but the charcoal lines were definitely branches.

Jihan smiled in self-mockery. Superstition was contagious, it seemed. In any case, he had dreamed of no foolishly grinning figure waving at the bound man.

Only then did it strike him how unlike Waldis was the man he had dreamed.

Domene, yes, but black haired, younger, thin. No one he knew. He sighed. Merely a figment of his imagination, which in its way was as overwrought as the flibbertygibbet's.

Once more, and finally, so much for visions. Probably the drawing had suggested the bound arms to him, but he simply had not marked that impression while he was awake. He refolded the paper and returned it to his pack, stripped himself to his nightshirt, and blew out the candle.

As his head touched the pillow he remembered who had been upstairs the night of the meeting. It was Poke who had cried, unable to find his mother. They had called for Marcy and she came down the stairs.

He had thought Marcy feared him. But what if her fear was of speaking to him? Or of being thought to do so. But then, if it was Marcy who had made him the drawing, did it have any meaning at all?

Did it have anything to do with why she died?

Could it have some meaning he had still not managed to grasp?

~ 14 ~

Skrying

he air stinks around you two," I say. They look at me ugly.

"Not for Garnet, is it? I say.

They're wondering could they cut me down if they tried. The fools.

"Not for Tanglevine, so don't pretend it," I tell them. "He's peerin' into your little games, ain't he?"

"This don't concern you. Tanglevine's not your people."

"Are now." I plant my feet wide, stick my hands in my pockets, blocking their way. It's just a flaunty pose to egg them on. While they were thinking of our argument I put a little turtle in each of 'em. If they reach for their knives, they'll move too slow. "Don't kill the Domene."

And Bandor does go for his knife. I let him draw it, then push my palm out, shoving with all my will. It falls out his hand. I smile.

"Don't kill the Domene," I repeat. "Bring him to me."

Jihan woke later than he intended. Light streamed through the east windows of the public room, speckled with leafy motion. Only the riders were there, sitting at the end of the table nearest the open door.

"Make ready to ride," he told them. "I want to leave within the hour. Where is Windland?"

Arn swallowed his hard boiled egg as if it might be taken from him. "He went out."

"Where?"

The riders shrugged.

Jihan looked hard at Arn, who only asked, "We're goin' to Song Becks'?"

Arn, at least, knew more than he was saying, of that Jihan was certain.

For now, he did not push. "Yes. Supposedly, we go to repeat the last of the Assessor's inspections and complete the replacement for his missing records. Of course, we actually have a more pressing purpose. At Song Becks' farm two loose ends dangle strangely nigh one another. Whether the Assessor ever left that farm alive is a question Song's behavior and her Coves in-laws' has raised from the beginning. And bear in mind that Song's husband Bandor Coves fathered Marcy's child."

"I managed to set near him last night," Camellia said. "He asked that friend of his all about you."

"Did he? They spoke of Windland too, did they not?"

Camellia nodded. "They think you and Windland's asking too many questions."

Jihan heard the hardness in her voice and knew the savaged child would not leave her thoughts, either. If getting the truth took harsh means, she was the one he would enlist.

"Today, Bandor Coves will answer every one of my questions," Jihan told her. He drummed his fingers on his sword hilt. "Where *is* Windland?"

Arn pushed a basket across the table toward him. "Try these, Ward."

It was half full of eggs, hard boiled and peeled. Some were tinted faintly yellow, some orange. "More satisfying than yesterday's mess, that's for sure."

Tal stretched in the sunlight. "What is it about Diddie's cooking?" He glanced to make sure the innkeeper was not in hearing to take offense. "It always leaves me hungrier than before I ate."

"Way she waters everything down," Arn took another egg from the basket. "It's a wonder we don't all have the runs."

Jihan bit into an egg. Its white was creamy and its yolk firm and fresh. "Fortunately, she has found no way to dilute hard boiled eggs." He finished it and took another.

"Ain't Diddie's. Sky brought 'em."

The last swallow went down like a rock. "What gives them their colors?" He thought of the orange fungus growing on the rotten trees by Tanglevine Creek.

Arn grinned. "Not poison. I ate four."

Jihan frowned down the rider's cheekiness. "What of the bay?"

"He's walking good, not favoring his foot. But if he was mine, Ward, I'd ride him easy today, see how he goes."

In that case he would need another mount to Song Beck's. He fixed Arn with his eye.

Steps sounded on the porch. Windland entered, and with him the old witch. Jihan tensed with annoyance. Sky strode to the table and peered into the basket. "Like my eggs, do you? Have more, they'll make you big and strong." She grinned up at Jihan.

Windland helped himself to one. "Yellow and orange marigold petals." He smiled at Sky. "Old family recipe? We cook 'em like this in my village."

"And we thank you for them." Jihan stepped between her and the caravan leader. "But now I must take Windland from you. We have business."

"We went to see the girl," the witch said. "Don't guess you care?"

"You're the healer." Jihan turned to the caravanner. "The drawing of Waldis in a tree," he said, "I know now who put it under my door. It was Marcy."

Windland's nostrils flared.

"It was she who went upstairs that night, remember? That explains its strangeness— neither quite childlike nor adult. She drew it with charcoal from the cooking fire. Maybe she knew nothing of Waldis' fate. My questions may merely have set her to imagining. But someone might have seen her leave it for me, and feared she knew."

Arn frowned. "Then why didn't they take the picture?"

"Perhaps she got it under my door first. It was locked. Besides, since she could write me no words, the greater threat would be Marcy herself, and what she might say. Tragic indeed, if she really knew nothing."

"'Course she knew something," Sky interrupted. "Marcy had sight. She had it strong." She sighed in exasperation. "What's this picture and why didn't you tell me about it?" she asked Windland.

The caravan leader did not answer her. So he had kept the knowledge of the drawing from the witch. Given an order, he had done his duty scrupulously. That was reassuring.

Ignoring the old woman, Jihan told him, "I made the right choice after all. Marcy is leading us to Waldis."

Sky crossed her skinny arms. "Well, of course it's all connected. Why else would the dance for Marcy drive that cousin of hers to raving about Waldis? But that poor girl ain't the one that hurt Marcy and Poke."

"The dance?" Jihan frowned. "What has that to do with the girl's raving?"

"What I said, Master. Or is it Ward?"

"Either. Are you saying your grand-daughter's dance caused the girl's fit?"

"You know good and well what that dance was."

"An illegal ritual."

Sky grinned so wide a gap showed where a side tooth was missing. "Right, Master Ward.

Now you're going to help us with another one. I need Windland, but I need you even more. We'll scry in the water to see who killed your tax man and Marcy."

Jihan had not the slightest notion what scrying was, nor did he care. "I've no time for children's games. Windland, we have work to do."

Sky unfolded her arms. "Take you to a secret place. The place you suspected my neighbors left off your map. Gonna ask for a vision in Lost Creek."

Jihan started. "Lost Creek is a real place? I thought it was only a metaphor for death."

"Can't it be both? It's also the place you dreamed about last night."

"I dreamed of no stream last night," Jihan retorted, stepping toward her. "Why did the villagers hide this Lost Creek from me?"

"'Cause it's a bad place," the witch snapped. "Didn't Windland tell you that?"

Jihan glanced at the caravan leader, but he was avoiding taking sides, merely chewing his egg and watching the exchange wearily. "He told me some old wives' tale about the creek becoming a dragon," Jihan said.

"Dragon, plague, storm, call it what you want. All that's bad about Tanglevine Creek flows into it from Lost Creek. Everything wrong with Tanglevine, soil, weather, water or woods, flows from Lost Creek." The old woman smiled scornfully. "But don't worry, we won't go near the worst of it, just a little ways to a quiet pool I know. Stay with us, don't drink the water and you'll be safe enough."

An idea occurred to Jihan. "This witchcraft of yours will reveal the killers' identities? Definite identities, I mean, names or faces?"

Sky looked him in the eye. "I give you my word as a healer. Lost Creek's got the answers you want."

His first instinct was about to pay off. The old woman knew something and had finally decided to reveal it. Even if she was still stringing them along, he saw a way to gain. "If I leave Lost Creek without at least one killer's identity clear to my satisfaction, will you cease all involvement in this matter and not approach Windland again until I say our work is complete?"

The caravanner glanced at Sky. He showed no apprehension, but Jihan sensed it.

The witch never broke gaze with Jihan. "We got a bargain."

"Then you have two hours."

Sky's mule stood saddled outside the inn. As she assured them the ride would be brief and effortless, Jihan took his bay. They followed the path westward down Tanglevine Creek.

Jihan attended to his mount's gait, paying little mind to the witch's explanation of scrying, the supposed art of seeing visions in a crystal, a mirror, or water. No hesitation was apparent in the bay's footfalls. Through his spine and thighs Jihan sensed no imbalance in its walk.

The last house in the village stood alone, a sturdy log dwelling with a pointed roof. Just beyond, a boulder more massive than the house jutted into the stream.

Sky reined in her decrepit mule. "My house." Through the open windows Jihan glimpsed bunches of tied herbs hanging, but no sign whether the dancer also lived there. "I guard the mouth of Lost Creek," the witch continued, "like my mama and grandmamma before me."

Windland laughed. The echo sounded against the boulder and the hillside. "We been coming and going past Lost Creek all along? You fooled me good."

Sky grinned. "I got me a few tricks."

Jihan saw no Lost Creek, only a wooded hillside, the tall grey boulder and Tanglevine Creek at its foot.

Sky flicked the end of her reins at the massive rock. "See it now, Master Ward Commander?"

Water curved around the boulder as well as beside it, Jihan realized. Another stream flowed into Tanglevine Creek from beyond the boulder. No magic was needed to realize that.

Sky kicked her mule and it slogged knee deep into the stream, skirting the rock. As the bay followed, a narrow ravine came into view.

Vines clung to its damp rock walls. Rivulets trickled among them, falling into Lost Creek with varied musics. Lights flickered on the water and on a faint trail along its right bank. On the mud between the trail and stream butterflies sucked, opening and closing their wings like leisurely fans.

"This is Tanglevine's terrifying secret?" Jihan asked.

"This is it." Sky smiled back at him, her long braid snaking over her shoulder.

"And its history?"

The old woman shrugged. "Used to be an outlaw hideout. It's seen some killings."

The path curved around an old tree with a trunk like a cluster of columns. A curtain of vines hung from its branches. The swaying tendrils brushed them. Beyond, the stream fell over a lip of stone. Above this was a small pool, a bowl of rippling light and shadow.

Sky crossed below the pool, then jumped off, climbing beside the falls while her mule wandered as it wished. Windland dropped his mare's reins in a grassy patch. Jihan knotted his flighty mount's reins securely around a low branch.

Putting a finger to her lips, the witch chose a soft hummock of moss at the pool's edge and knelt there, signing Windland and Jihan to sit on either side of her. The pool reflected tall trees upside down, and blue sky brindled with clouds. A fine sight—for those with nothing better to do than admire it.

"Don't talk unless I say," the witch murmured. "Just sit restful, both of you, and look at the water. Windland, you know the questions. What happened to your tax man, who killed Marcy and Poke. Domene, if patient concentration's beyond you, just hush and sit. You don't have to understand. Just by being here you're helping, take my word for it."

The witch drew in a slow breath and relaxed.

Gazing into the pool, she let her breath out slowly. Windland's eyes skimmed the water's surface, but she elbowed him and shook her head. Her eyes reflected the water's shimmer, seemingly focused on neither the surface nor the bottom. The caravan leader stilled his gaze, letting it, too, unfocus on the water.

Jihan tried doing the same. He saw branches mirrored there, a rock bed beneath, and a few minnows.

Quietly, the witch began humming. Like the villagers during the dance, she wavered to no particular tune or rhythm. Had her voice been melodic, its mingling with the little waterfall might have soothed. Jihan tried to make use of the time to reconsider the Becks, the Coves, and what Marcy might have known, but the witch's humming prickled like red ants crawling over bare skin, distracting him.

She leaned forward, veined hands on her knees. "Look," she whispered. The water reflected a bird winging between the treetops, two clouds that gradually drifted into one like an indistinct hat with a lopsided plume. A minnow nibbled at an empty snail shell.

No one would trust Marcy with dangerous information. But she might have overheard or witnessed something. Was that why she feared an inspection? Had she seen an inspection lead to a quarrel, and death?

Sky was silent. A leaf landed on the water. Ripples slowly spread, perfect circles blooming one within another, calm and shining.

He wondered where Mirabil was, what she was doing. At this hour she might be conferring with the housekeeper, or the steward of their Gatelands cultivation. Or if she planned to go out, selecting a robe to please and impress the other wives, perhaps her simple cream silk, with her hair in the pearl clasps he had given her. He imagined it swept up, shining like rose gold at the white nape of her neck.

What occupied her thoughts at this moment? Not him, he suspected. Once they had been inseparable. But now? With the boys, the rivalries among the Wards' wives, the management of the household and land holdings, her life was full. And it was entirely within the Caverns.

They had known it would be so, at least for a while. Both of them came from Outlands Administration families. Once they had thought he would eventually succeed his father as Master of the Outlands and sit on the Council, rarely traveling farther than the Gatelands immediately above the Caverns.

Now no such smooth path lay before him. He must take this chance. Yet, he could not have them in Arcadia with him. The boys must be educated in the City. Would he never again be more than a passing visitor in her heart? Jihan gazed up at the leaves. He owed too much to his sons to indulge in yearning. He owed too much to his unjustly defeated father.

He owed too much to Mirabil herself, who had married a future Councilor but now found herself the wife of a mere adventurer.

The clouds gathered into sluggish curdles, not quite textured, not quite a blur. Pockets coalesced like ears and a mouth, a bar of shadow like a single broad eyebrow. A Coves eyebrow.

"Bandor," the witch whispered.

Jihan turned quickly, but she gazed into the water, unaware of him.

"'Eah," Windland agreed. "Got himself a knife."

Jihan peered where they were looking. He saw only a small, pale crayfish.

Sky sucked in a breath. "Curved or straight?"

"Jaggedy."

The witch tensed. "Same as I see. But what's he doin' with it?"

"Using it," Windland whispered. "Stabbing."

"Stabbing who? We need to know!"

Jihan moved restlessly. All three of them disliked Bandor Coves. His reputed ill treatment of the murdered girl and child, his guilty skulking, his crooked partnership with Able Lasts, too easily led to facile notions of Bandor quarreling with Waldis, Marcy discovering his guilt, Bandor silencing her. But ripping open the chest of his own two year old son? The reasoning simply did not hold.

"Water," the witch mumbled. "Lost Creek?"

"Blood," Windland corrected. His blue stare was as empty as a cup of tinted glass.

"Fancies," Jihan answered.

Sky frowned at the water. "Tree."

Windland nodded agreement.

"You see a tree? Astonishing!" Jihan glared at the foliage surrounding them, hemming them in, clinging spider-like to the ravine walls above them. "Your time is up."

"Not yet," the witch's unfocused gaze did not waver.

It was true that two hours could not have passed, but he'd had enough. Jihan rose and strode past the horses, his jaw tight with mounting anger. Tree, indeed. Blood. Jaggedy knife. Baby talk. Meaningless. As meaningless as

Marcy's drawing, Waldis in a tree singing like a bird, a man waving with a silly grin.

A meaningless grin.

As meaningless as Able Last's grimace, the distortion of his nervous twitch. Hastily Jihan pulled Marcy's drawing from his pocket. The charcoal was getting smeared, but the smile of the figure on the ground was lopsided, one side of the mouth pulled much higher than the other.

That was it. The figure on the ground was Able. And as he looked up at Waldis hanging bound to the branches, he was not waving, he was menacing. It was not Bandor Coves who had reason to fear Marcy's drawing.

It was Able Lasts.

~ 15 ~

Lost Creek

pside down their two reflections peek back at them. What their reflections see, I see. Clouds crown their heads, their eyes are mirrors, their thoughts drift like dreams in the water. Dreams that coil into nightmare.

What will our Domene do now? He sees, but what? Does he hear what they say? Fire to their water, whirl of fierce will, he rushes the brook like a bull, stoops like a hawk on two finches, a one man cavalry charge. He grips Windland, shakes him out of his dream, leaving him exhausted and bemuddled.

Poor Cousin Windland's been through too much. Half moons are dark beneath his eyes. It's telling on him, what I'm taking from him.

Only, he can't stop yet. I need more.

Maybe his life.

So you let him be, Jihan you impossible hornet swarm!

Ha, look at Sky give our fine lord what for, tell him how dangerous it is to snap the trance laid by my creek.

Windland just shakes his head, trying to rid it of the colors of my pool. He's a strong dreamer, stronger than he knows.

"There is no time!" The Domene accent rings against the rock walls. He unties the bay, leaps on and he's already dashing like Frogtown Race Meet. Don't ride so breakneck, handsome Jihan. Your horse is like you, too proud to know when he hurts. As for you, you disaster, you silly dollop of flame, you churning inside the hard belly of a jewel, do you have any notion what's lurking for you? What craves to have you?

This is what we wanted, I remind myself.

This is why we need him, our cock-a-doodle Domene.

It's going right well.

Only, now he's alone. Now he's left his guide behind, and the witch, and I'm not that strong yet.

He thinks he's the hunter. Thinks his sword and his battle skill can help him. Thinks he's after that old thug Able.

He's blind. He's naked to the Storm.

"Saddle up," Jihan told the riders. "We're taking Able Lasts in for questioning."

Arn came out of a stall, curry comb in hand. "Where's Windland?"

"Playing at fortune telling with the witch."

The other riders had paused from their grooming and cleaning. Arn asked, "She got him in a trance?"

The concern in the rider's dark eyes was far more than he let show in his voice. He deserved an answer. Jihan told him, "I know little of such matters, but I think he was in one and is now recovering. Come, we are wasting time."

Arn reached for his bridle, and the others moved into action. Jihan unfolded the villagers' map. Able's farm lay in the hills north of the village. In fact, it might be near Lost Creek, though he knew nothing of its upper course.

Why had they made such a fuss to hide the stream? The witch's explanation was hardly convincing. But the most direct route seemed to be a trail at the far end of the village. It climbed the hills northeast to another farm, then cut northwest to Able Lasts'.

Wordlessly Jihan showed the route to Arn, then pocketed the map and mounted.

A fine drizzle dripped from the leaves. From the smithy and houses a face or two watched curiously as they passed girt with their swords and knives.

The path into the hills was easily found. At once it began ascending steeply through oaks with the rain spitting against their foliage, and cedars exuding a dark fragrance.

"Marcy believed Able killed the Assessor," he informed the riders as they traveled two abreast. "Whether she was right I don't know, but I do know that Able, more than Bandor, wants your leader out of the way. I heard Able tell Bandor that Windland's work with me is a betrayal. How, then, might he react to Marcy's attempt to inform on him?"

"The way she and the little'un was killed, and the way Able twitches," Camellia said. "Think he goes crazy?"

"Where I come from, twitching's a sign of possession," Tal answered.

Camellia nodded. "Last night that girl was possessed."

"Let us not run away with that," Jihan stopped them. "Whether or not violence drove Able Lasts to madness once he started, too many signs suggest Marcy's killing was reasoned. I believe that if we can discover his reason for committing this crime it will lead us to Waldis."

He glanced over his shoulder at Camellia. "Whatever it takes, Able will talk."

She nodded, her scarred face showing no qualms.

They passed a clearing with ramshackle farm buildings. The way veered northwest along a ridge, then zigzagged down the other side. The bay stumbled, but recovered and sped on, hooves beating a steady rhythm on the damp earth. A scramble up a rugged slope brought them to a high, rocky place open to the sky.

Rain blew in their faces as they overlooked a level upland planted with crops, and a wooden dwelling with a roof of baked tiles. Nearby stood a barn of timber as yet unweathered.

"Looks like ol' Able does well," Arn remarked.

"There he is." Jihan pointed out two figures in the yard, small in the distance. He was certain of the taller one.

The path plunged down into the woods, cutting off the view. The farm was less than a mile away, Jihan judged. Silently he cursed the steep, slow going, fearing they had been seen, that their quarry would evade them.

Finally the trees thinned. The house and barn stood before them. The gate was open. A few cows grazed in a field. Geese milled in the yard, but no other two legged being was in sight.

The geese honked as they drew up before the house, spoiling any hope of surprise. "Watch the back and barn," Jihan told Arn and Daw as he dismounted. Signaling Camellia and Tal to follow, he drew his sword and ran up the porch steps to the door. He threw it open.

They entered a sitting room furnished with heavy chairs, a large hearth, a woven rug. Across an inner doorway lay Able Lasts.

Blood darkened the floor boards around him. "No," Jihan protested through clenched teeth, but Able's hands moved, closing on the handle of the knife that protruded from his chest. He was still alive. Jihan knelt by him. "Don't pull it out," he warned. "You may bleed to death."

Able's eyes moved toward him. His head turned more slowly. "Been bleed anyway. Inside." From the labored bubbling of the breath he drew, he was right.

"Who stabbed you?"

"The witch can stop the bleeding." Able grasped Jihan's arm with a bloody hand. "Get her!"

Tal rose. Jihan stopped him with a look.
"First, answer three questions. The first two are
simple. Who did this, and why?"

A tremor jerked the fingers clutching his
arm, an incongruous quickness as if they played
a stringed instrument. Able Lasts' mouth
stretched in what might be a twitch. Or a smile.

Jihan wrenched him up by the shoulders.
"Who?"

"Bandor," Able cried out. He tried to worm
away, but had to fight for breath. "Let me lie
still."

Jihan propped him in the door frame,
hoping it would keep him from drowning in the
blood filling his lungs. "Why?"

"You know why, damn you to torment—
that's why you're here." Able panted, blood
oozing from around the knife.

"Why?" Camellia demanded.

Able's gaze met hers. "For Marcy and her
brat. Marcy tried to tell you, didn't she?" He
coughed. "Bandor didn't want to—but I called
up the Storm. Should of seen him then!" He
grinned at her.

"Bandor helped kill them?" Camellia
whispered, stricken.

"Bandor killed the boy. His own little'un."
Able's laugh was obscene, blood and derision

clogging it. Jihan gripped the gaping jaw, forcing
the dying man to look at him. "You've answered
two questions. One more. What happened to
Waldis?"

Rain blew against the window glass. Able's
grin was a rictus of pain, but he made a small,
triumphant sound. He was reveling in the power
death gave him. Even now he would escape, and
he knew it. But he wanted to speak. He fought
for breath. "We got your tax man, Bandor an'
me. Bandor took him back to the stay, like
Diddie been tell you—but we lured 'im out. Took
him—took him up Lost Creek. We carved him
up nice and slow. Curse of Tanglevine took your
tax man." He coughed. Blood bubbled from his
mouth. "Want Bandor?"

"Yes!" Jihan answered.

"If I know Bandor—been hide—Torran's
Well—at the headwaters. Go on, catch him." He
laughed in Jihan's face, flecks of blood flying.
"Witch's spell gonna get you too—Bandor's
gonna cut you—watch your innards work." Rain
battered the windows, but the noise seemed to
augment Able's whisper. "Gonna slit open your
heart and poke his finger inside."

Jihan shoved him down. Rushing to the yard
he called the other two riders. "We are after
Bandor Coves."

"Found his tracks," Daw answered. "He went in and out the gate on horseback."

"Ride westward."

"To where?" Arn asked.

Jihan put his boot in the stirrup. "Lost Creek."

Arn made no move to mount. "No."

Jihan froze. "What did you say?"

"No," Arn repeated, squinting against the rain. "Not to Lost Creek. Windland's orders."

The others stood by their horses. It was clear they would follow Arn's lead. Even Camellia. Jihan took his foot from the stirrup. "I said ride to Lost Creek."

The scrawny rider pushed his wet hair from his face. "Windland said no."

"You are willing to face court martial for him?"

"Yes, Ward."

Jihan narrowed his eyes, scenting the kill. "But would you condemn Windland? If we lose Bandor now, I will charge Windland with treason."

"*Treason*? It's not treason!"

"Does that matter? I can do it, and I will."

Arn's gaze faltered. He realized it was no bluff.

"Mount," Jihan commanded. He sprang into the saddle, wheeled the bay, and galloped for the trail. The riders' horses sounded behind him. It took no skilled tracker to see the fresh hoof marks denting the mud of the trail, climbing a ridge, then descending toward Lost Creek. Jihan jabbed the bay with his heels. Able's laughter gurgled in the rain as he sped after Bandor Coves, the riders at his heels.

"That must be it." He drew rein. A new trail lay before them. It followed a seam in the land, almost narrow enough to leap a horse across, but deep. Through the treetops below he glimpsed water.

"Bandor went upstream." Camellia pointed to depressions in the sodden path.

"As Able said he would." Jihan urged the bay forward.

Light split the sky. Thunder crashed as if the blow tore open the earth. The bay screamed and bolted, branches lashing, blinding Jihan. He felt the horse lurch, hindquarters slipping, then he was slithering downward, clinging to the mane as his mount struggled for footing, found it at last, and stood trembling with terror.

"All's well," Jihan reassured the animal, letting it feel his hand firm on the reins, though he too was shaken and panting.

Gathering his wits, he called out for the riders, but the wind and rain carried away the sound. Trees whipped and creaked around him as the rain became a downpour. He had no idea where the trail was, but he was all too aware of the rushing stream below. It was rising in its narrow bed.

Returning as he had come was impossible. The horse could never make that climb, but he did not want to descend farther. Aside from the flooding, he would change from the hunter to the prey if Bandor was on the path above. He saw no solution but to pick slowly along the steep hillside, hoping to find a way up.

At first his choice seemed right. The bay shuddered as it stepped carefully among the roots, but withstood the crashing thunder, taking comfort from his voice. If horses had likes and dislikes for particular riders, he did not think this one much liked him, but they were in this together.

The rain stung like gravel, and the gloom deepened, though sunset must be hours away. The steep ground ran like a river. At last, the inevitable happened. The little shelf of land he followed shrank. Ahead was only the vertical side of the ravine.

The only possibility was to return. He muttered a curse, then coaxed the animal to collect itself and turn tightly. He had one consolation. If the deluge had immobilized him, it may have done the same to Bandor. If the killer had been forced to seek shelter the riders might catch him.

He gave the bay a word of praise for its neat turn and pressed his calves slightly. The horse set its hoof on a mass of decaying leaves. Jihan felt the shift in the pit of his stomach as the ground slipped. The horse heaved with all its might, but the trail gave way. The mudslide took vines and saplings with it, crashing over them. Snatching his foot from the stirrup, Jihan flung himself free in time to avoid being crushed as the bay went down.

He fell, branches tearing his skin and hair. He managed to grasp one, only to feel his arm gripped and wrenched loose. Able's grip, he thought as the water roared up to meet him, the same quick roll, like fingers playing a stringed instrument. Then the cold torrent of Lost Creek took him.

~ 16 ~

Wasted Time

ihan shivered as he pressed a clean cloth to the gash above his right eyebrow. Despite the fire in the hearth and the dry clothes he had put on, he was chilled to the bone.

"Could've killed my riders," Windland told him coldly.

The riders? They had merely searched unsuccessfully for him, then gone to the inn for help. They had not even attempted to capture Bandor.

"Probably did kill your horse."

"*You* dare criticize?" Jihan rounded on him. "When I needed backup, you were unfit for duty. Now we have another murder and the killer goes free. Why? Because your riders hesitated. You had them disobey direct orders."

"Just one."

The cloth was already soaked with blood. He flung it into the fire and took another from the stack Diddie had laid ready. Holding it to his brow, he glared at the caravan leader. His struggle with the flood had been a journey alone through hell. The battering force of the water and stones, the danger of being dragged under or knocked out, these he could fight. Well he knew how joining such a battle turned fear into exultant desperation. But helpless terror now reverberated through him, unlike any fear he had known before.

Maybe the mudslide on the solid-seeming trail was only weather, but what of the grip he had felt as he fell, what of the hatred of the flood that loosened his hold on rocks, pried roots from his grasp, what of the weight that pushed him beneath the water and held him until his lungs were a burning torment and his body writhed, controlled by a will not his own?

To be overmatched, utterly powerless, with no hope even of knowing what or whom he fought—that he could not endure.

It was despair, and he never wanted to feel it again.

In the end, mere luck had saved him. Hurled against a cleft tree, he had managed to drag himself from the torrent. As his head cleared, an irony mocked him. He was huddling by the same pool where the witch had done her nonsense— or so he had thought her magic this morning. Now it was a perturbed expanse of opaque mud-red, identifiable only by the tree with the vine curtain, the strands of which tumbled madly in the water.

"Should I ask Sky to see to that cut, Ward?" Arn suggested, setting a mug of beer by him.

"That you will not," Jihan growled. He drank and turned back to Windland. "The villagers would not draw Lost Creek on the map. That night, you gave them permission not to. You ordered your riders not to take me there. Why was I kept away from Lost Creek? What is concealed there?"

"Nothing Arcadia wants. Don't you feel by now that Lost Creek is best let be, Commander Jihan?"

"Something assailed me there. Something that cannot be, but is. A hatred with hands and a thinking mind."

That rag too was wet with blood. Jihan threw it at the fire and pressed another to his forehead. "Just as I cannot explain how Bandor and Able killed the girl and child without leaving a trace on the muddy ground. You have been talking about a curse. *Curse of Tanglevine took your tax man*, Able Lasts taunted me. *Witch's spell gonna get you too.*" He fixed the caravan leader with a close scrutiny. "You would have told me more, had I not scoffed. I am not scoffing now."

The caravan leader regarded him silently. "I can see you're not," he said at last.

"Then tell me."

"Tell you what?"

"You Outlanders live at nature's mercy. For that, my people think themselves superior to you. But when the Great Disasters drove my people to take shelter in the Caverns, yours suffered with the animals and land. You survived by learning from them. You and they grew close—look at you and your horses. I do not believe your people have supernatural powers. But I begin to think you can sense, even direct, some of the forces of nature in ways we Domenes do not understand. Is it not said that in old times your witches used these forces as weapons?"

Windland regarded him, the straight brows slanted in a slight frown. "Fine words," he answered at last, "but they're over my head, Commander."

Jihan pushed the cloth hard against his throbbing forehead. "I think not."

"You've had a rough time," Windland said, "hurt your head pretty bad. Maybe your imagination's a little excited? Sky means us no harm. Able and Bandor are vicious but too dumb to pound sand. That's the size of it."

For days Windland had tried to make him see. How could he deny it all now? "The size of it is that the rain has eased, I've had enough coddling, and Bandor is still on the loose." Jihan rose, fighting dizziness.

"Even if you had a horse, we can't search in the flood."

"No need to search. He's at Torran's Well."

Windland showed not the least startlement at that. "Able said? You trust Able?"

"I see you don't deny it," Jihan accused.

Windland shrugged. "With respect, a clearer head, rest, and daylight will be good for us all." Rising, he strolled to the riders and Diddie's elder son. "Dice, two coppers up?"

Jihan moved toward him in anger. The room spun.

Camellia looked over. "He's right, Ward Jihan. Rain may be ending, but the flood won't be."

"'Specially up Lost Creek," the innkeeper's son added.

Jihan found the end of the other table before him, and sank down on the bench. They were right, and he knew it. "When?" he demanded.

"Locals know their own creeks best."
Windland glanced at Diddie.

"After a rain like we've just had, say six
hours for Lost Creek to drop," she answered
apologetically. "That is, if it ain't been rain again
tonight."

Windland stretched lazily. "If Bandor's up
the gorge he's either drowned or stuck wherever
he took shelter. He can't travel anymore than we
can." He took two coppers from his pocket and
put them on the table. "Who's in?"

Jihan removed the cloth. It was stained but
not soaked. The bleeding was lessening. He sat
watching them all narrowly. Head wound or no,
he was imagining nothing. Windland and the
locals shared some secret of which even the
riders were ignorant.

The riders were outsiders to this province.
Windland was a stranger to the village, yet his
tattoo was known. To these people, it marked
him as special. He, or his family, carried some
authority here.

And Jihan guessed well enough what it was.
This province's old religion had gone
underground, but had it really died? Could it,
when it was part and parcel of their mysterious
collusion with their land? Not unless they forgot
all that they were.

That they had done so was a lie for official
reports. Arcadia knew better. For three
generations, Arcadia had ridiculed local superstitions but bent Domene law to avoid conflicts.
The Council Master had warned him, had he
only listened. What was Windland to these
people? A scion of the old, disinherited,
chieftains? Was that why it was a betrayal for
him, in particular, to work for the Domed City?

Or, from the very beginning, had Windland
Wisteri been working for his own ends?

Morosely, Jihan watched the riders toss the
dice. If he were on the run like Bandor, with
seasoned hunters after him, he would not wait
for dry going. Even with what he now knew of
Lost Creek in flood, he would put distance
between himself and his pursuers. Bandor must
realize his only chance lay in getting a head start,
in flying to the Eastern Mountains beyond
Arcadia's reach. Then, Jihan knew all too well,
Bandor would escape him.

Windland smiled as he raked in the coins.
Pushing one into the center he rolled with a
graceful flick of the wrist.

It was not that the caravan leader sided with
the murderers. Windland and Sky had thought
Bandor guilty before he himself had. Or, had

learned it from the water? Bandor with a jagged knife. Blood. It was Able's killing they had seen.

But did Windland care whether the murderer faced justice? Nothing suggested he did. Or that he cared at all about the murdered girl and child. Two farmers trudged in, removing dripping jackets. The caravan leader scooted over to give them room without so much as glancing to check the weather.

Did Windland want this expedition to fail? Since their arrival in Tanglevine—no, even before that—he had withheld information, done nothing of any particular use, and today had hampered Jihan's every move. Windland and he respected one another's skills, and Jihan saw now that he had let this lull him.

Had he been played for a fool? The caravanner was not ignorant of Domelands politics, nor of the frontier war. Did Windland suspect his intentions in the Blue Grass?

In that cold light, was it not possible that the man was doing all he could to misdirect him, to snare him into failure?

More steps clattered on the porch. Diddie's younger son burst in. "Your horse," his voice rang shrill with excitement. "Master Jihan, Dogwood Lissa's found your horse!"

Hurrying out, Jihan saw a lantern, and motion between the trees. As he went into the drizzle he saw a woman holding the bay by the bridle, and a little girl lighting the way.

Its eyes rolled, its mane and tail were matted with twigs and mud, and the leather of its saddle was all but ruined. It bled from scrapes and cuts, but those did not look deep. "Saw 'im streakin' across my bottom land at dusk," the woman said. "Been take me this long to catch 'im, that's what a mischief he is!" She patted the wet neck.

"I am deeply in your debt." Jihan took the bridle. The bay jerked its head, but walked evenly when led.

"Must do your heart good to know the scamp's come through it."

"A near miracle, after the fall we had." The bay repaid the woman's care by aiming a kick at her child. Jihan turned it sharply, forcing its weight onto that leg.

"Careful," he warned. "Its adventures have not improved its temper." He handed the reins to Windland. "Check its condition, you and Arn. I trust in your incomparable skill," he said, taking sour pleasure in ending their dice game. Leaving them to it without a backward glance, he thanked the farmer and paid her well for her pains.

All was quiet in the public room with no rattle of dice and little conversation among the locals who had been drawn by the lights and noise of the horse's return. It was good to regain a valuable animal, but he would be happier if it proved able to ride out at dawn.

"Beer?" The innkeeper asked. Jihan pushed his mug forward and she came over with her pitcher. "Our dancer sent a message. She offers to entertain for a fee."

He looked up. "Oh?" A more welcome diversion from the dragging time could hardly be imagined. The cost did not matter. "It amuses her to involve an Arcadian official in prohibited rituals?" He smiled, removing the sting from the reprimand.

"Just a dance this time." Diddie smiled back. "Just for pretty, as we say here."

Jihan took back his filled mug. "Let us have it."

A few more villagers wandered in, got beer and sat quietly, the old witch among them. Apparently, she had taken the word around.

An old man entered with a triad of hand drums, one with jingles like a tambourine. Tucking himself onto a stool by the embers he began patting out a rhythm in varied pitches, spiced with occasional jingling.

Sipping his beer, Jihan awaited the other musicians.

The dancer herself whirled in.

No ceremonial white drapery this time. She wore a dress of emerald green, silk by its shine and supple flow. She never got such rich cloth in this village. She must have bought it in the horse country, and must have the means to afford it—not surprising, considering her skill.

She swept the gathering with her glance, smiled, and lifted her chin. At the drums' light roll, her body began to sway. Her coppery hair rippled down her back. Her shoulders were bare, tanned the hue of honey, her collarbones small and fine. Green fringe made her sinuous movements shimmer like a forest pool in leafy sunlight. As she stepped sideways Jihan saw her skirt was slit up the side—so far up that when she turned the honey colored skin of her right thigh was bared to the hip. The revelation lasted a mere instant, leaving every man in the room fervently hoping for a more vigorous turn. She smiled, knowing how enticing beyond all reason a mere glimpse could be, when it was a stolen glimpse.

As the drums' tapping sharpened she opened her arms, her hips tipping in response. Diddie had been right, this dance was no more mystical than any tavern dance in the Gate City, but it was far more charming. Well did this dancer distinguish between sensuous delight and crudity. Her breasts and hips lifted to the drum beats as if they were the sound itself, too elusive to be flesh and muscle. They were small breasts, her body lithe and fine as Jihan liked best. Her glance met his, and he smiled in appreciation.

The warmth of her answering smile eased the tension in his back. Between his uneasy days in Tanglevine and his disturbed dreams, it had been too long since he had felt simple pleasure.

Hair streaming, she spun, legs flashing, revealed a hip slender and strong, eyes lighting on him with each turn.

He found himself toying with a fall to temptation. Wishing to. Resisting it.

Of course, she knew who was paying, whom her dance must please, but he did not mind that. He enjoyed her dancing for him, displaying her agile beauty and skill for his pleasure.

Women often tried to interest him, drawn by his wealth or rank, and maybe the dancer was no different, but that hardly mattered. Rarely had he felt such a need for simple relief as he felt tonight.

With a wild motion she threw back her head, arms stretching, body arching into a back bend that bared her leg, her thigh, her hip, came tantalizingly close to baring more. She struck a perfect balance between delicacy and sensuality, equally arousing frustration and throbbing hope, a heightened intoxication poised on a knife's edge.

Jihan fell, once again drowning, but this time in a perdition of desire.

She straightened. Shook out her hair. With the dignity of some legendary queen she strolled to the rude trestle counter. Diddie drew her a mug of beer. Catching the innkeeper's eye Jihan nodded that he would pay. Possessive gratification filled him that it was he who slaked her thirst. The dancer glanced over her shoulder. To his delight, she made for his end of the table.

Her breathing was quick from the dance, her cheeks flushed. "Thank you." Her voice was light, soft edged like Windland's, the accent of the province's heart.

Jihan smiled. "Beer would be a poor acknowledgement for such artistry."

Her blue-grey eyes looked full into his. "Later for that."

Jihan considered, and liked his conclusion. He gestured courteously to the bench. She perched beside him, nimble as a bird, draping her emerald skirt gracefully over her lap. The smooth skin of her hip and thigh showed at the slit. The scent of her brought an ache to his chest that beat in his cock, his throat, the marrow of his bones. "You have lived in the horse country," he said.

"I was born there." She drank in quick swallows like a child.

"Where?"

"Upthegrove."

"Why bring such skill here? Is it not in demand in the towns?"

She smiled. "Why bring yourself here? You're too fierce and fine to chase village thugs."

"It has to be done."

"Nobody ever tells you what to do, do they?" she asked.

"What makes you think not?"

Her eyes were serious, as open to his gaze as Windland's. "Every sound and move of you."

"But you have seen little of me."

"More than you think." She smiled, teasing him. "I watched you before you saw me."

Intrigued, he asked, "And did you like what you saw?"

She tipped up her mug. When she lowered it he saw nothing of the child about her. "Do you know the Comilan story of Lucifer? No, I don't like what I see. But oh, you're beautiful, Jihan the Domene."

Triumph filled him. "Come. I don't wish to share you with the others anymore."

She shook her head, laughing softly at him. "No."

"You said I am beautiful. Is not Lucifer desirable?"

She smiled.

"I will have you."

"Maybe." She set down her mug beside his, both empty. Closing a hand around each he looked to the counter for Diddie to refill them. When he turned back, the dancer was gone.

The loss came sharper than a blow. He searched the room with an eager gaze, but could not find her. When Diddie came he indicated only his own mug.

She would not return, and he knew it. He had pushed too hard. He had needed her warmth, the comfort of her sensuality, too much. He stood, taking his beer with him. "Wake me an hour before dawn. The riders, also."

He did not bother to light the candle. Throwing his clothes at the foot of the bed in empty frustration, he cast himself on the hard mattress, condemned to hot, leaf-rustling insomnia.

~ 17 ~

Fern

A floor board creaked. Jihan turned to face the door. The shadows of two feet darkened the crack of light beneath it. Taking his dagger from beside the pillow he rose and flung open the door.

The dancer stood there, her hand raised to knock.

He felt ridiculous.

She looked at his nightshirt, the knife. "I woke you?" Beneath a soft cloak of pale grey she still wore her dancing costume. Another dream, an apparition invented by his need? But she blocked the light from the hall, solid and real.

With a gesture he invited her in, though he was all too aware of the stifling heat, mosquitoes and rude bed with its rumpled sheets. "I can offer few comforts, I fear."

"A door to shut out the world. A quiet place. It's enough." Taking the candle, she lit it in the hall, then she did shut out the world and barred the door against it. Nothing existed but the small room, and the woman surrounded by a ring of light. She turned, her candlelight catching the silvery glitter of the sash draped over the chair. "Pretty." Her eyes moved down to the glint in his hand. "Pretty too. Can I see?"

For a moment he distrusted. But all the reasons for that were banished beyond the door. He laid the dagger on her open palm. Putting the candle on the night stand, she held the knife between her fingers by its pommel and point. The gold and garnets in its hilt sparked embers in her eyes, on her face. She seemed a priestess of some ancient, bloodthirsty mystery, her lips moving slightly as she whispered to the weapon. But what she told it was, "Never hurt my people."

None too pleased, he swooped it out of her hands and put it in his pack.

She glanced at his sword in its scabbard leaning against the wall. "You took the little one and left me the big one," she teased.

He smiled. "Should I fear?" Unfastening her cloak he drew it off and flung it over the chair, revealing the litheness of her body in the thin costume, the points of her nipples that responded to the friction—or to his nearness?—quickening his heartbeat and turning the throbbing in his head to sweet singing.

She frowned, her straight brows slanting into fierce lines. "You have another one hidden on you."

"Another weapon? None, I give you my word."

"You know right well you do."

Following her glance downward, he saw what she meant. "That," he admitted. "Well, then. Do you dare to disarm me?"

She stepped to him, laying her open hand on his racing heart. "I lied, too. I do like you, Jihan Domene. I like how I can embarrass you but I can't outface you. I like that if you had to fight the whole world empty handed, you wouldn't complain. You'd just do it. I want to spar with you...but I'd rather touch you."

Her fingertips explored his cheek, his beard, the lines of his brows and nose. Their gentleness eased three raw days of suspicions and betrayals.

"Sky says there's no hope for you. She says you love only yourself." Her hand returned to his chest, her eyelids lowering as if to listen. She whispered, "She's wrong."

He pulled her to him. Through the silk he stroked her supple back. Smiling, she brushed his hair back over his shoulder and raising on her toes, she kissed him. She tasted like morning rain. Jihan lifted her in his arms, carrying the grace and beauty of her to the bed.

He laid her there, her hair spread on the pillow, and marveled at the exquisite creature he had captured. Every part of her was a study in delicate strength.

Her desire was as magnificent as she was, her cheeks flushed in the candlelight, her eyes and parted lips eager, innocent of awkwardness, or shyness, or guilt, or any of the sly calculation he associated with her kind. In her abandon she was as simple as some wild woodland creature, accepting him as she found him, meeting his gaze honestly, openly, as if the look were a handclasp between them, or many days' intimate knowledge. To exchange this gaze was almost enough.

But the time until dawn was too short. He kissed her parted lips, gathering her to him as he gave chase to her tongue with his, then retreated until she sweetly ambushed him. Gently she nipped his lower lip, found the outline of his upper lip beneath his moustache. This made her laugh softly. He avenged himself by holding her down, tickling her throat with his beard and the edges of his teeth, down to the green silk. A single clasp somewhere held it all and he searched for it, found it at her side, bit it, growling over the impediment like a savage dog. Smiling, she reached to unfasten it, but he pinned her arms, working it loose with his teeth and letting her feel the beast the untamable openness of her wakened in him. Taking her dress by the side slit, he laid her bare whether she was ready or not.

She was. Looking into his eyes, she arched to him. He felt her body taut beneath him, the skin of her thigh and hip under his hand, her breasts pressing his chest through the cotton.

"Hand over that nightshirt, Jihan with the wonderful lips and river jade eyes. I'll throw it in a corner and have all of you for mine. You with your boldness and your daring like fire, and your poor, hurt forehead—does your head ache?"

He kissed her collarbone, a fine slant like a wing. "No longer." His lips followed the swell of her breast. "Not since you walked through the door."

He took her nipple between his lips and sucked, feeling it draw tight against his tongue, its hardened bud a shameless eloquence.

More shameless still, her grip gathering his shirt. It slid up his thighs and with a shock of pleasure he felt his erection press the smooth heat of her skin. He moaned around her nipple.

The shirt was drawn up to his armpits and her fingertips skimmed lightly over his bare back and downward, learning every shape of him they could reach.

He pulled away long enough to strip off the nightshirt and toss it as far as she had wished.

Raising over her, he pushed her down, greedy to see all of her. The nipples of her small, supple breasts were seashell pink and peaked with desire. Indentations slanted from her slender hips to hair as fiery as a maple leaf and as elegant in shape. But over her lower left side and hip curved the tattoo of a heron wading in a swirl of water.

She touched his face, raising it to meet her gaze. "What's wrong?"

"That." He pointed, trying to keep the sharpness out of his voice.

"Some of us decorate ourselves. We think it's pretty. It's just color put under the skin with needle pokes—"

"Yes, but why that design? What does it mean?"

"Heron's a Sun bird. He flies up the creek in the morning and down the creek at dusk. Some birds come and go with the seasons, but the heron always stays on his creek, watching over it."

"Like the witches?"

"Only some of my kin are witches."

"Is Windland a witch?"

"No."

"Before the war, your clan was the chief priest's clan."

Eyes serious, she reached up, her fingers gliding softly through his hair. "Does it matter either way now? To us?"

Her earnestness, her vulnerability as she lay beneath him, her hair rippling over the pillow, her eyes alive with the wholehearted wish that he would not pull away, showed him what a fool it would take to pursue it.

If he was right, so what? So the old witch resented him and the caravan leader's loyalties were divided. Was that a reason to throw away all that she offered him? The bird decorating her body did not mar her beauty. What had seemed outlandish on Windland's male body increased the elegance of the woman's, the bird's sinuous neck and breast curving over the inward and outward flow of her waist and hip as if twining around her in a graceful embrace.

"No," he told her. "The past matters nothing, nor the future. This time is ours to shape as we will."

She smiled. Her fingertips traced a dance of
fire over his body, scratching sensuous claws
through the hair on his upper chest, then she
lowered her head to taste him, licking greedily
down between his ribs. The unpredictable
sharpness of her teeth heightened the pleasure
of her lips and tongue as she invaded his navel,
bit and sucked downward until his cock strained
and he moaned with craving. But her nails
grazed him where the hair grew dense again
below his navel

"Impatient," she whispered.

He snarled, thrusting himself into her hand.
Instead she cupped his balls, surprising an eager
cry from him.

"Yes," she whispered, closing the other
around the shaft of his cock. It leapt in her hand,
throbbing so insistently that he grasped her,
forcing her down. Holding her at his mercy, he
pushed her thighs wide open with his knees.

She moaned as she looked into his eyes. The
current that coursed between them was stronger
than Lost Creek, more absolute than its flood.
As he plunged into her she locked her arms hard
around him, urging him. He cried out at the
pleasure of her legs fiercely clasping his waist.

Lithe as some sinuous vine she twisted and
rolled with him, and her secret depths

undulated, capturing him, caressing and
tormenting him with delights beyond endurance,
arching to push him out only to open and coax
him deeper in.

With soft kisses and sharp nails she urged
him to drive faster, harder, to open yet deeper
desires in her and claim yet sweeter pleasures.
She withheld nothing from him. She keened her
ecstasy in a single high cry, his name.

It pierced his heart. He felt the outrush of
his tenderness with the surging of his cock.
Beyond all considerations of reason or other
loyalties, he embraced wholly whoever she was,
whatever past lay behind her, whatever the
future could or could not offer them. His heart
beat with hers as he lay blinded by the mingled
copper waves of her hair and dark of his own,
content just to hold her.

"I wish I could stay with you all day and far
into the next," he murmured.

"I know. You mean to ride soon as the water
gurgles down."

He shaped his hand to the curve of her hip.
"I have no choice."

"Your chest hair makes a triangle." She touched one of his nipples, the other, kissed the hollow of his throat. "You're a geometry."

"And what are you?" He laid his open hand on the soft curls and gentle swell of her sex.

"A shape that fits with yours."

He smiled. But he was honest with her. "Leading to a geometry problem. I've a family, and work to accomplish. I wanted only to prevent an incident over the Assessor's death, then go quickly to Arcadia. Now what I want complicates that."

"No, it doesn't."

"Not among your people, maybe. But among mine—"

"You'll see." She circled his navel with her fingertip. "You can be in the Fortress by tonight. If you get your tax man's body and his killers are dead," her finger traced downward, "and all's calm between your people and mine," her hand opened, following the indented line of muscle to his groin, "you'll already play from a strong hand at the Fortress, won't you?"

"Mmm." He arched his hips slightly, inviting her to keep touching.

"Then you've won. There's no need to ride up Lost Creek."

He stretched lazily. "Why not?"

"Able Lasts is dead. Bandor Coves is dead."

"We don't know about Bandor."

"I see Bandor. You forget I'm a witch."

"I don't forget." He smiled at her. "I am under your spell."

"And I'm under yours," she answered seriously.

"I have no magic. That's your people's specialty."

"Isn't this the strongest magic of all?" She closed her hand around his cock and laid her other hand on his heart.

"Maybe so," he admitted, opening his hands likewise on her. He felt her heartbeat and his own. "So the flood killed Bandor?"

"The Storm did."

"This Storm all of you speak of, it's no mere weather, is it?" He turned onto his side to face her. "It has a mind. I felt it."

She was silent. For a terrible moment he thought she would deny it, as Windland had done. But she frowned. "Don't know I'd say it thinks. But it senses. It hates. It wants."

"What does it want?"

"You."

Startled, he laughed. "Come, now. If these hills contain some evil, what can it know or care of me?"

"It may not know your name, but it feels what you are. Killing you would make its circle whole." She watched him, troubled. "And, my beautiful Jihan, it won't kill you kindly."

"So I've gathered. But, why me?"

"You've guessed by now it used Able and Bandor to kill your Assessor. And Marcy when she tried to protect Bandor and point you at Able. You know that Waldis wasn't the first. It started way long ago. Ninety-three years ago."

"At Torran's Well."

She nodded. "Then, Tanglevine had a witch named Fern. She was born in my village."

"And of your family?"

"Yes. Fern was thirteen when the Domene soldiers marched into Upthegrove. Three hundred of them, hauling people from their houses, burning everything. They killed Tyree— the one you called the 'chief priest.' He was her uncle." Her hand tightened on his arm. "They killed her aunt, her cousins—one was her sweetheart she would've married. Fern was no witch yet, she could do nothing to stop it. She could only watch helplessly as they were murdered."

Jihan listened quietly. He knew the incident. It was an ugly one, but belief in the chief priest and his oracles had inspired decades of resistance. Within a year of his removal and his heirs', the Blue Grass was a Domelands province.

"Fern grew up in hard times. Domene soldiers running up hill and down dale doing whatever they wanted. She 'prenticed herself to the best witches she could find. She wanted to learn enough to drive the Domenes out of the Blue Grass." She shrugged. "Silly girl. As soon try to magic away night, or cold weather, or death. Even Domenes probably have some purpose, but she couldn't get that through her head. What she'd seen had made her a little crazy, maybe. But she got powerful in her way. She settled in Tanglevine because it was so far up in the woods they hardly ever bothered it. In those days life was easier here than now, and people lived better.

"One day, a tax collector came from the Fortress. Torran, his name was. He pushed his weight around, took double what was due. Had a farmer flogged for standing up to his ways. Flogged to death. Then he threatened a couple of village toughs who hadn't reported all their property."

"So, they killed him," Jihan guessed. "Like Bandor and Able. History repeating itself."

"But not quite. Fern smelt their plan. She didn't mind one less Domene bully in the world, but she needed—she thought—to make herself so strong that nobody could threaten the ones she loved. She had a man to protect by then, and a baby girl. She had Tanglevine to protect, and all the Blue Grass. She told the two toughs she'd cover for 'em if they'd bring her the Domene and let her kill him her way."

Jihan raised on his elbow, frowning down at her. "She bound him in an underground spring," he said. "She tortured him to death, cut him open, split his heart. He was a thin man with jet black hair."

She nodded, unsurprised. "You dreamed of him. Did you see his blood flowing into Lost Creek? That was Fern's creek where she lived. She drank the water and blood. Drank all the power of his life, his anguish, the unendurable jolt of it when he died. She did gain power. But most of the blood went into the creek. Her spell gathered all her pain and hate, all Torran's meanness and torment, all kinds of suffering the war had brought to the land and people. She made a thing she couldn't control. It hated what she hated, but no love was in it, only hunger to guard and destroy. That's the Storm. And the plague. Plague wiped out most of Tanglevine. It killed Fern's man."

"But not her child. She was your ancestor, wasn't she?"

"Deer, Fern's little'un, grew up. Deer had a daughter, too. That's Sky."

"No wonder your grandmother is such a sour old woman. And Fern?"

"When Fern saw what she'd made, when she came face to face with it, she realized the evil she'd done. She tried to fight it, and it turned on her. Plague killed her. She crawled into the spring cave, hoping her death would satisfy it and lay it to rest. Torran's bones are hidden somewhere in the hills, but Fern's bones lie in Torran's Well."

Jihan was silent, wondering what to believe. The tale made a kind of sense of his dreams, of Waldis' disappearance and Tanglevine's curse, but were such things possible?

No. They could not be.

"Now you see why this is my fight, not yours," she told him. "I'm the one who's riding out. You're an Edwars, your great-grandfather ruled the Domed City during the war. See now why it craves you? Why taking you would make its circle whole? *Don't you see that your coming to the Blue Grass is what woke it up?*" When he didn't answer she grasped his shoulders, shaking him. "Listen to me, Jihan. The things it would do to you!"

He took her arms, holding her off. He considered her sadly. She was sincere, desirable, trying to help him.

But she was mad. Maybe all her people were, but her madness pierced and wounded him.

"I go to challenge no sorcerous entity," he told her. "I hunt only a human fugitive. I must bring him to trial or account for his death."

"But Bandor's not up Lost Creek. Something worse is! If it takes you it'll grow too strong, then nobody can stop it—"

"Calm yourself. Listen to yourself. Can you not hear that's madness?"

She tried to free herself. "In Tanglevine, you're the one who's crazy. You're a bull blundering through a village dance, you don't know the steps, you can't even hear the music!" She flung herself backward. He let go. She landed against the footboard, small breasts heaving with her labored breath. "Many's the time I'd smacked you upside the head, *hard*, if I hadn't done an even more ridiculous thing and loved you," she said.

Sitting up, she pushed her hair out of her eyes. With a visible effort she lowered her voice. "This is my business, and Sky's, and Windland's. We're Wisteri. The Storm is Fern's fault, and ours to mend, if we can. We thought you were our bait, to draw it out. But now you've given me what I need."

"Meaning what?"

"All I need to fight the Storm. You opened to me, you gave me your passion, and your sweet tenderness. You made me love again. Your fire burns in me, I have you inside me." She laid one hand on her sex, the other over her womb. "I have enough to lure it now. I thought I needed you, but I don't."

The flood had him again, dragging him down, down. "That's what you wanted from me? My semen? For your witchcraft?"

"Don't be stupid—"

"For some test of your magic?" He took her costume, shoved it into her arms and threw her cloak around her. Pulling her to the door, he thrust her from the room and banged the latch shut, his head throbbing. She pounded on the door, shouting something, but pain tore his mind from his senses. He could not hear her.

At last, raising his head, he saw a hint of grey at the window. It was almost dawn. He began to dress.

~ 18 ~

The Hunt

He had not heard her footsteps, but she was gone. All was now silent outside his door. Jihan tugged on his boots, loathing the well-being that glowed through him. It was physical merely. She had preyed on his loneliness in this alien place. Disoriented, his sense of reality assailed, he had yearned for companion-ship and trust.

It had made him easy prey.

Well, the gain was not entirely hers. His body's needs had been satisfied, at least. Now he had a job to do. He thrust his dagger into his belt and buckled on his sword.

This sense of loss was unreasonable. He hardly knew the woman. Nor was he free to love her, even had her feeling for him not been a lie.

But it was a lie. Had she seduced him honestly, bargaining for some costly gift or political favor, he might have accepted gladly in his loneliness.

But she had not bargained, she had robbed him, and what she had stolen he would never have bartered away. Not his semen, to hell with that. She had duped him of far more. What he had given to her so unguardedly he had given to very few in his life. To her it was only fuel for some witches' power struggle. Duplicitous, all of these people. None were to be trusted. They did nothing straightforwardly.

So why did the thought that he would never see her again give so much pain?

He drew his sword. As always, his nerves thrilled to its chill metallic timbre. He checked its keen edge. Perfect. Lethal. Reliable.

Magic existed, he had been forced to acknowledge that, but were these provincials really attuned to mysteries he did not understand? Or after all, was magic no more than the power of suggestion? Face to face, was not a good blade always far better? He sheathed the sword, ready.

Even love for a stranger was only power of suggestion. Some exerted it unconsciously—love at first sight. She had intentionally imposed it on him. But it was only an illusion. Soon it would fade. The old witch, her grandmother, also had such powers, making Windland see Bandor in the pool.

What of the third Wisteri, Windland? He was not a witch, she had said, but he had similar abilities. Those uneasy fancies in the woods even before they entered Tanglevine—it was Windland, not he, who had feared the journey.

And those imaginings that the caravan leader was some primeval expression of this land, some elemental—Jihan was not given to such flights of fantasy.

Nor was he some diviner to dream the prophetic nightmares that thronged on him here.

What of the most mysterious of his dreams, old Sky's firelight spell, and Windland offering himself to the ghostly heron? The meaning of that dream still puzzled him, if it had one.

Why had the caravanner given himself to the blue fire's embrace? Just as the witch-dancer had given herself to him. The heron's sinuous coiling around the caravanner reminded him of nothing, aside from the tattoo. And the grace of the dancer in her white veiling.

Jihan's hand went cold on the hilt of his sword. How alike those two were, the caravan leader and the dancer. In looks, in agility of body and mind, in the accents and rhythms of their speech, they seemed not distant cousins, but twins. Had Windland been female, he might almost have been the dancer.

Jihan shuddered. That could not be.

He had bedded a woman. He was sure of it. His head wound had not befuddled his wits so much as that. Nor was he going mad. He vividly remembered her supple breasts, the slender softness of her body, the plunge into the female core of her and its yielding, rippling grip on him. He knew a woman from a man!

But how much did he know of magic's illusions? Nothing, since he had never believed in them until now.

Why could he remember the taste of her kisses, but not the female scent of her?

What of Windland's flirting in the stable? What of Arn's pack and hat by Windland's bed? Why had Windland been so disinterested in the dancer's beauty? He had not even bothered to come in for her second dance, though old Sky had.

Why did the dancer only appear when Windland was absent, and he only reappear when she had gone?

Vertigo opened beneath him. His dizziness grew at this new distrust of his own senses. His gorge rose at what he might have unknowingly done.

I have you inside me. I have enough to lure it now.

That was exactly what Windland wanted. To fight this ancestral curse he believed in. Since the night Sky had recruited him, his only real efforts had gone into that.

No, he would not believe it. Curse or no, he had a murderer to catch. Over this, at least, he still had control. If Bandor was alive, he would take him. In Arcadia he would force Bandor to reveal the truth.

The entire truth.

Jihan slipped his sash over his shoulder, knotted the fringed ends, and went out. He banged loudly on Windland's door, then the riders', rousing them. Passing the cold hearth and craving coffee, he stepped out to the grey dawn. Cool mists from Tanglevine Creek coiled beneath the dripping leaves, but already the humidity was closing in. The heat would soon press heavily.

The bay dozed in its stall, tired but with no swelling or heat that Jihan could find, and it had eaten its grain. As he saddled he heard the riders enter and begin to do likewise. "He should rest," Windland said from the stall door.

Jihan did not turn toward him. "You found nothing amiss?"

"He's tired."

"There is no other horse."

The caravan leader did not answer, but Jihan sensed him lingering. He cinched up and let out the stirrups, ignoring him, but what he yearned to do was seize the crop and strike the man across the face. When he at last turned to lead the horse from the stall, Windland had gone, as silently as the dancer had.

The trail began behind the village, branching from the path he and the riders had taken to Able's. Jihan led, with no choice but to place Windland next to him, since Windland knew the way to Torran's Well.

"We'll strike Lost Creek upstream of where you were yesterday," the caravanner said. "The way down's marked by two trees grown together, Sky said, big ones. If the water's gone down, we'll find Torran's Well a mile upstream."

Jihan grunted assent without turning to him. They negotiated the steep ups and downs as quickly as the slippery going allowed, brushed by wet branches in the growing dawn. Young and spirited though it was, the bay was weary. As they turned onto the path above Lost Creek it was blowing and its ears were back. Just a little more, he thought, patting its neck encouragingly. It was less willing to accept his comfort than yesterday.

Below, the water raced, filling its banks, but only to the brim. The lower trail showed between the trees, muddy but no longer submerged. Nothing now hindered Bandor's escape.

The double tree loomed, two trunks that had twined so long ago their bark had fused. Two kinds of leaves sprouted from its wet blackness. Just beyond, a steep path led downward between pines strewn with creeping vines.

The birds silenced as they descended, sliding on the damp pine needles. They could no longer see the bottom of the ravine. If Bandor passed below they would not know it until they saw his tracks.

But when they reached the stream, no hooves or feet marked the mud. Lost Creek rushed noisily through a narrow bottomland, its high grass beginning to lift from the swath left by the flood. The heavier weed stalks still bent to the damp earth. Full morning had come, but all was grey and silent except the water.

The reins jerked through Jihan's hands as the bay stumbled. It righted itself, but the next step was uneven, and the next. The horse was lame. As Jihan dropped back and the riders passed him, Windland rode on, tense and upright in the saddle as if all along Jihan's control had been illusory, and this hunt had been his. "Halt," Jihan called.

To his surprise, the chestnut stopped. But Windland did not turn in the saddle. He stared at the path ahead as if he feared to look away from it. "I need your horse," Jihan told Arn.

Hooves sounded behind. Jihan wheeled, drawing his sword. An iron-dark horse trotted from between the pines, slender like its rider. She wore rough pants and a brown shirt, but her coppery hair flowed long.

The dancer.

Relief loosened Jihan's joints. Ahead, Windland dismounted as she lit from her saddle. "Fern," the caravan leader's relief sounded as strong as his own, but her clear eyes, greyer than Windland's, were dilated with the same fear Jihan saw in the caravanner's.

~ 19 ~

The Storm

Steel echoed as the riders sheathed their swords. Windland handed his reins to Camellia and started up the trail on foot. "Fern?" Jihan said, but her gaze was on Windland's back, or else on the path beyond him. For all she noted Jihan, he might have been a stone.

But as she passed him she laid her hand on his chest. "Stay back," she whispered. For a moment, her palm rested over his heart.

Then she passed him. Arn stepped into the way, blocking Jihan and the other riders. "We wait here."

"He might need us," Tal protested.

The circles beneath Arn's eyes were nearly as marked as Windland's. "We wait here."

Windland and the dancer disappeared beyond a thicket of young trees. Shoving Arn out of his way, Jihan hastened after.

If there was danger, he could not see it. Only a curve of racing creek, the swath of wet grass, trees with their branches weighed down by water. Even the birds and insects seemed to have deserted Lost Creek.

The two ahead walked close together, hand almost touching hand, but it did not seem the closeness of lovers. They were comrades guarding one another.

The path skirted a rocky outcrop, concealing them again. What ailed him that he could not catch them up? What had become of his will? But whatever this journey was, Jihan knew he no longer commanded it. Rounding the outcrop, he heard crows.

Heavy wings flapped among the leaves. Raucous caws hailed the three of them, calls less of alarm than rancor and derision. Jihan recognized only too well the odor filling the steep sided valley.

Ahead a wall of tangled laurels rose, and pines above that. Where laurel roots shadowed an overhang of damp limestone, Lost Creek issued from a deep recess. Torran's Well. But as Jihan caught up to Fern and Windland, she pointed at the wooded hillside.

In the branches of a tree a man hung, arms stretched as if flying. The tatters of a velvet robe hung on him and his long hair was grey. He had been killed as Jihan saw in his nightmare. As the raving girl had taunted, the crows had taken Waldis' eyes, and much of his face.

They had been at his exposed vitals as well. As the witch Fern had once killed the tax collector Torran. "There," she said quietly. "Take him, and go back to Arcadia."

"You had no hand in it?" Jihan asked, sick with dread of the answer.

Her eyes widened as if he had struck her. Windland stepped between them angrily.

But she laid a restraining hand on his arm. "It's a fair question. No, Jihan, I had no hand in this man's death. I tried to stop them, but I wasn't strong enough."

The stench and the boiling of the creek from its dark spring made his head swim. "But you lied about Torran. When did you kill him? Five years ago? Ten?"

"Able's dead," she answered. "Bandor's dead, I give you my word. Now leave this place—quick!" She turned to Windland. "Make him go."

"Make him?" Windland gave her a droll look. But then he shook his head regretfully. "Even if I could make him do anything, I wouldn't. We need him."

"We don't. You know why."

"That might not trick it." Windland's quiet voice was matter-of-fact, implacable. "It wants him. If we can't lure it now, we may never get another chance."

"No. I won't—"

With a black rush the crows filled the sky. They wheeled, cawing an alarm that echoed through the ravine, and fled. Touching Fern's shoulder, Windland pointed.

On the hillside before them, pine branches stirred. Nothing else moved, but Fern closed her eyes, taking a deep breath. The sound of blowing leaves grew. The lashing of the branches spread slowly from tree to tree, strange in the windless valley.

Fear tensed Windland's face, but when Fern opened her eyes she was calm. Without consultation, she and Windland moved forward toward the mouth of the creek, taking positions prearranged and known to them both. Where a sapling and larger tree stood a little apart Windland placed himself in front of her. Taking hold of the sapling's trunk and a hanging branch of the tree, he stood between the woman and the slowly advancing disturbance in the branches, his arms spread as if to shield her.

The commotion grew in violence as it descended the hill. Laurel leaves loosened and whirled. The water flowing from the spring cave faltered, clogged, then burst into the air. Jihan drew his sword but remained rooted where he was, at a loss. Nothing could he see of any assailant, nothing could he hear but the turbulent wind. The motion of the leaves and grass approached the two who stood between him and Torran's Well. The roar filled his ears.

The dancer raised her arms. Her light, high voice rose above the noise.

> "I stand on my own ground,
>   My bones are this ground.
> I stand in a ring of fire,
>   Time is my fire.
> Four stars flame in my circle,
>   North and South are closed to you.
>   East and West gates shine against you.
>   This water no longer holds you!
> The dance of life unbinds you,
> The circling stars burn you away!"

The bending of the grass rushed toward her. Windland's hair blew back and his shirt billowed. He glanced back at her, terror in his eyes, but Jihan could feel not the slightest stir of air, and not a hair lifted on the dancer's head.

The sky darkened. Trees heaved as if struggling to free themselves. The ground rumbled beneath Jihan's feet as if thunder rolled through caverns below. He felt a thickening of the still air around him, more nauseating than the corpse's stench. The pressure was the malaise that had weighed on them as they viewed the storm's damage, the flies that had fed on Marcy's death and the child's, the hatred he had heard in the girl's raving and in Able's laughter, the force that had dragged him beneath the flood, destroying his urge to live.

Fern spread her hand wide, tracing geometries, but leaving each of them open. "Loosen! My woven spell, unweave! Unravel! Scatter! I made you in darkness. Now the stars eat you and turn you into light!

Leaves were ripped from the trees. Waldis' corpse jigged in mockery of her dances. Windland's head snapped back. He gripped the sapling and branch, fighting to keep the shield of his body and will between the Storm and Fern.

She answered the onslaught with a dance of her own, a circle on the grass, but she left it incomplete. "Think you're strong, you old empty bag?" she taunted it. "Death is an eye blink! You killed me, but look at me!"

Windland's body jerked as if from a lash. He cried out as it struck him. Fern's voice rose high and fervent. "You're a mistake made in a dark time, that's all!" Windland arched wildly under blow after blow, slipped on the wet grass, but regained his footing. The shield he made endured.

"Butterflies live on Lost Creek now," Fern defied the Storm. "Look in my heart. Go on, look—what do you see there?" Sensing some change, she laughed and raised her hands. Water clashed in the creek bed. Lifting, it curled upstream, opposing the buffeting of the Storm. She threw back her head to chant the final spell.

Windland screamed, straining rigid. He clawed desperately, but his grip slipped and with a broken moan he crumpled to the ground, as still as death.

The Storm howled. The flattening grass rushed past Fern straight for Jihan. Wind struck him. He raised his sword, but the rending force offered nothing to strike. Quickly the witch faced him. Her voice rose, chanting, but the roaring of the Storm drowned it out. Jihan could scarcely see through the spinning of the vines and branches. The vertigo claimed him with a triumphant howl. He slashed and slashed at nothing.

The whirlwind reeked with the taste of Waldis' putrefaction. With every breath, disease filled his lungs. It crammed the pit of his stomach and came up, rushing through his limbs to erupt in scalding sores.

The sword fell from his shaking grip as foul lesions multiplied on his hands. Tumors bulged on his nose and brows, and leprous disfigurements reshaped his lips. He could no longer close his eyes against the horror of himself, his eyelids were gone. He screamed, but his throat was blocked by he knew not what.

He did not want to live. Not like this. Sinking to his knees, he awaited the stroke that would cleave him, bare his beating heart.

Fern flung up her arms. Blue fire danced incandescent along her fingers. Jihan's vision cleared a little. He felt the Storm waver and lessen as its attention shifted to her.

He could blink his burning eyes. His hands closed, sensation tingling in fingers that had not, after all, been eaten away. He struggled up from his knees. His will was no longer in its grip. Despair no longer possessed him. The Storm was now intent on Fern. Giving a shout, she reached for it with blue fires flickering in her eyes.

It no longer paid any heed to Jihan. The way was clear behind him, the riders and horses waiting. Nothing stood between him and escape.

With an enraged roar the Storm wrenched Fern into the air and flung her against a tree trunk. Pieces of bark and twigs swarmed into her eyes. She cried out, twisting in blind pain and clawing at her face.

He had no reason to die with these two who had deceived him. This hunt of theirs had nothing to do with him, he had not agreed to it, did not understand it. Jihan stooped, cautiously reached for his sword. Oblivious to him, the Storm howled around the witch. He pulled the sword to him, sheathed it.

Fern crawled, groping. Jihan felt its hatred of her. Maybe it could not kill her, but it would devour her. It would drive her to despair, fill her with its foulness. Then it would take Windland. Already it had Fern. Her blind eyes stared, all black pupil, voids leading into empty darkness.

Fury filled Jihan. He launched himself at the invisible thing that gloated over her. *"You will not destroy her!"*

He placed himself between the evil and the two of them.

Behind him, she moaned. He heard her grasp the tree, pulling herself to her feet. "I belong to the Sun," she whispered.

A tremor went through the ravine. The Storm swirled, uncertain which of them was its prey, or which the greater danger.

"You had better kill her if you want me." Jihan told it. "But you must kill me to get to her." He smiled, mocking it. "A geometrical dilemma, is it not?"

"Your rising is beautiful in the gate of the sky," Fern whispered behind him, "living Sun, beginning of life."

The branch behind creaked as Windland staggered up. Breathing hard, he stumbled forward and put himself between the Storm and Jihan. Jihan joined him, sharing the brunt of it with him. With their arms they made an unbroken circle around Fern. Hands clasped firmly, Jihan and Windland protected her as she chanted the final banishing spell.

> *"Hate born of love, love born from hate,*
> *North and South welcome you,*
> *East and West gates open their light to you.*
> *The circling sun unbinds you.*
> *You open your heart to joy.*
> *Free, you rise and fly to the Sun!"*

~ 20 ~

Gone

here is she?" Jihan asked. "She said she would join us."

Sky set plates of cornbread and bacon on the table before him and Windland. Her kitchen smelled strongly of herbs, many familiar and unknown scents mingling. "She lied."

The caravanner gave the old witch a sharp look. "Maybe not. *Death is an eye blink,* she said."

The wood of the kitchen table had a rippled grain. It swam like a queasy sea. Some of the light headedness was lack of food, Jihan knew, but he was not hungry.

Sky wiped her hands on a dish towel. "Well," she admitted thoughtfully, "I grant you that one. But it'll be right long before you see Fern again. Maybe all the way out the other end of time."

"Your granddaughter is not dead," Jihan answered in cold anger.

"Foolish boy. You don't understand even yet, do you?" Sky pulled out a chair and sat down. "I never had any children. That's my grand*mother* you're in love with."

He understood. It was only that he could not accept it. She could not be gone forever.

"Ease off," Windland told her. "If it wasn't for Jihan the Storm would've had us."

Sky was silent. At last she grudgingly allowed, "Fern's at peace now. If you love her, take comfort you did that for her."

Jihan clenched his jaw, willing his eyes to stay dry, not to betray him before the old witch.

"Know what?" Sky continued to Windland. "First time around, it was Able who killed Bandor. Marcy outlived Bandor. Able killed her and the boy, then himself. They—it—cheated and that nearly worked. Knowing the past didn't warn me what it would do next."

Windland nodded. "Fern said Bandor and Able were laughing about it."

"Taking turns killing each other? Just a joke, I guess, for ghosts."

With an effort, Jihan raised his head. "What? Bandor and Able were dead too?"

"All Tanglevine was ghosts. Even the geese and pigs." Sky pushed the plate of food at him. "All 'cept me and my ol' mule, Tulip. I told you, I'm this place's guardian. I keep foolish people and critters from straying into it. Or, I did." Wonderment came into her voice. "Guess my job's over."

Jihan fought to still the spinning of the room.

Sky turned to Windland. "You saw the village wasn't real soon as you rode in, didn't you?"

"I knew there's no Tanglevine anymore." Windland cut a slab of cornbread in half and put bacon between the pieces.

Jihan regarded him wearily. "You knew all along?"

"I knew something had to be wrong, and it scared me. But I didn't want to say too much till I knew what was going on. Didn't really know till Sky told me."

"The night Fern came to you in the shape of a heron?" Jihan asked.

Sky glanced at Windland. "He sees too much," she muttered.

"Only because of Fern," Windland answered.

"Fern didn't give a peediddle about him yet."

"We don't know that."

Jihan tried to collect his bewildered thoughts. Above the herbs hanging from the rafters, painted stars showed faintly on the ceiling. He focused his eyes on Windland again. "How do you know her thoughts? What was your joining with her?"

"Because we were kin I could help her. Sky had tried, but..."

"I'm just too damn old," Sky put in. "She needed more strength than mine to take a shape and hold it."

"The Storm woke Tanglevine," Windland continued, "but it tried to keep Fern out. It knew she'd fight it. She could see us, but she needed help to take a shape solid enough to seem real to you." He paused, then added quietly, "For you to touch."

Jihan looked quickly at him. "But you shared only your strength. You did not share her awareness."

"Some of it," Windland looked away politely.

Jihan forced his mind onto more bearable paths. "But what of Diddie?" he asked. "What of the farmers? You say the Storm raised them, but they were only ordinary, decent people, most of them."

"'Course, just themselves. I doubt most of 'em even knew they was ghosts," Sky said. "That's all it needed, to keep you occupied, and here, so it could decoy you out from under our guard."

"You see why I had to be careful what I told you," Windland said apologetically. "If you'd thought I was crazy, you wouldn't let me stay near. I had to stick-to you tight as a burr till Fern was strong enough to let you challenge it."

"I see that," Jihan returned. "Fern's duty was clear. She had to destroy it, whatever the cost."

"Yes, she had to," Windland said quietly, "but I was afraid. Something else got too important to her at the end."

Jihan met his eyes, and understood what he was not saying before the old woman. That Fern as he had known her was not the murderer she had once been, or tormented by remorse as she had become. She was Fern as she should have been. That in the simple accident of loving her enemy, she had found her salvation.

"But what waked the curse after all these years?" Sky asked. "Domene tax men have come and gone for a century." She considered Jihan narrowly. "When did you start out for the Blue Grass?"

Jihan thought. "Thirteen days ago."

The old woman turned to Windland. "Told you so." She faced Jihan. "What about *you* roused it?"

"We've been through that," Windland answered wearily. "He's the great grandson—"

"Fern wouldn't listen, but he's up to no good. He's got secrets he's not tellin'."

"Doesn't everybody? I'd say we're deep in his debt."

"You trust him because he saved your life?" Sky flapped her hand, brushing it away.

Windland looked at Jihan "'Bout time we start for Arcadia?"

"High time," Jihan answered.

"Watch your step, Domene," Sky muttered.

Jihan turned coldly to her. But the grey of her eyes, and a certain slant to her nose, stilled his anger. "Health to you." He rose and went out.

Tanglevine Creek flowed fast, joined at the boulder by the clear water of Lost Creek. Upstream through the trees, piles of rotted wood humped up among the vines, the remains of the smithy, the store, the stone chimney half standing above the fallen roof of the inn.

"He's learned things," came Sky's voice through her open window.

"I know," Windland answered.

"She thought that just because he saved her, she's saved him, too. But what he knows could make him more dangerous."

"Could make him the Domene we've needed here for a century," Windland countered.

Jihan walked through the trees, not caring what they thought. It was true, reconsideration was needed.

The Blue Grass was not what he had supposed.

Death was less than he had supposed.

Love was more than he had supposed.

"Free, you rise and fly to the Sun," he murmured.

The insects' shrilling rose from the hillsides, and a breeze rustled the leaves. Its gentle touch eased the raw ache a little.

About the Author

Born in Lexington, Kentucky, Beth Tashery Shannon holds an MFA in creative writing and has published experimental fiction in *Pushcart Prize* III and IX, *Chicago Review,* and *TriQuarterly Review. Twilight* actor Edi Gathegi performed her "Bons" with WordTheatre in 2009. Her short story in *Pleasures: Women Write Erotica* (Doubleday) was partial basis for an ABC TV movie.

Also with an MA in art history, she worked with the Egypt Exploration Society's excavations at el-Amarna and contributed to *Amarna Reports* IV and meetings of the American Research Center in Egypt.

Shannon's nonfiction also includes an essay on *Salome* in *Approaches to Teaching the Works of Oscar Wilde* (MLA Press). She has taught university creative writing courses and edited fiction for a publishing house.

Under the pseudonym Elizabeth Adair she is the author of *The Sun and Stars*, a mystery novel set in the court of Henry VIII (BearCat Press, 2012).

Currently she lives in Georgetown, Kentucky where she writes, designs books, and volunteers as a tour guide, researcher and back-scratcher-of-elderly-stallions at Old Friends, a retirement facility for Thoroughbred horses.

Discussion Questions

1. What is Tanglevine, a fantasy, a murder mystery or a ghost story?

2. Which character do you identify with the most, Jihan, Windland or Fern? Why?

3. Were the sections from Fern's point of view interesting or just confusing? Would the story have been better without them? How would the story have been different without them?

4. *Tanglevine* might be described as a story in which opposites interact. What oppositions do you identify in *Tanglevine*? How do these drive the characters' motivations and actions?

5. Through most of the story Jihan believes he is a detective in a murder investigation. At what point did you realize other things might be going on, and what gave you that idea?

6. Could this story have been told with a contemporary or historical setting, or is it inseparable from its setting?

7. At the end Jihan overhears Windland and the old witch Sky arguing about him. Windland thinks Jihan has changed. Sky thinks not and warns Windland that Jihan is dangerous. What do they mean? Has Jihan changed, do you think?

8. Did anything in Tanglevine reverberate with your own experiences or observations? If yes, how? If no, why not?

9. Did anything in Tanglevine make you uncomfortable? If so, why did you feel that way?

10. What themes do you find in Tanglevine? What does the author seem to have to say about those themes?

More titles from BearCat Press

Helen of Troy by Tess Collins

The Appalachian Thriller Trilogy
by Tess Collins:
The Law of Revenge
The Law of the Dead
The Law of Betrayal

The Sun and Stars by Elizabeth Adair

The Art of the Traditional Short Story
by Lester Gorn and James N. Frey

Floats the Dark Shadow by Yves Fey

Design

Cover and interior by Frogtown Bookmaker.

Great Blue Heron, Tampa© 2009
by Biswamberpal

BearCat Press logo by Golden Sage Creative

Eileen Caps font © 2003 by Dieter Steffmann

Flourishes: NeoClassic Flourons Free
© 2011 by Paolo W.

CPSIA information can be obtained at www.ICGtesting.com
Printed in the USA
LVOW041459050213

318758LV00003B/45/P